You're invited to a

CREEPOVER ™

Ready for a Scare?

written by P. J. Night

SIMON SPOTLIGHT
New York London Toronto Sydney

SIMON SPOTLIGHT
An imprint of Simon & Schuster Children's Publishing Division
1230 Avenue of the Americas, New York, New York 10020
Copyright © 2011 by Simon & Schuster, Inc. All rights reserved, including the right of reproduction in whole or in part in any form. YOU'RE INVITED TO A CREEPOVER is a trademark of Simon & Schuster, Inc. SIMON SPOTLIGHT and colophon are registered trademarks of Simon & Schuster, Inc.
Text by Heather Alexander
For information about special discounts for bulk purchases, please contact Simon & Schuster Special Sales at 1-866-506-1949 or business@simonandschuster.com.
Manufactured in the United States of America 0711 OFF
First Edition 10 9 8 7 6 5 4 3 2 1
Library of Congress Cataloging-in-Publication Data
Night, P. J. Ready for a scare? / written by P.J. Night. — 1st ed.
p. cm. — (You're invited to a creepover)
Summary: When Kelly and some friends have a webcam sleepover while her parents are stranded in a snowstorm out of town, Kelly tries to scare her friends with creepy tricks.
ISBN 978-1-4424-2903-1 ISBN 978-1-4424-2904-8 (eBook)
[1. Sleepovers—Fiction. 2. Snow—Fiction. 3. Horror stories.] I. Title. PZ7.N576Yo 2011 [Fic]—dc22
2011001384

PROLOGUE

At first, all she felt was the cold.

Each crystal of snow pierced her bare skin, stinging like an electric volt. A sensation so violent, so torturous. Frigid wetness seeped through the fabric of her pretty red dress. Her body tried to double into itself, to search for what little internal warmth lingered in this coffin of cold.

Then the coldness was gone. In its place a heaviness, a numbness remained.

She tried desperately to move but couldn't. The wet snow pressed on her body. Forcing her down. Pushing her on all sides. Unseen hands dragging her away, away from the light, from the air, from life.

Fight. She had to fight. *This can't be the end,* her brain screamed.

Desperately she tried to force open her ice-crusted eyelids, but the weight of the snow had created a mask, encasing her face, her head, and her body.

She concentrated on her fingers. It took every ounce of energy to connect her brain with her right hand, to will her knuckles to bend ever so slightly. She had to free herself. She forced her hand to move, to scrape at the icy blanket smothering her. But each little movement caused the avalanche of snow to press down harder. To bury her deeper.

She moaned, though she knew no one could hear her. Why had she come? Why had she listened?

It seemed impossible that across the yard, people were still drinking steaming mugs of hot cocoa, singing carols, and eating dainty cookies cut into precious holiday shapes. Only minutes ago she had been in the warmth of the house, part of her aunt's party, accepted, included.

Unfair. It was all so unfair.

She scraped her fingernails violently against the snow that encased her. Eyes sealed shut, she could visualize her red polished nails clawing at the bright white snow. Someone would pay, she decided. Someone would have to.

"Miss Mary? Is that you, Miss Mary?"

She shuddered as the voice on the phone echoed in her head. Why had she answered? She should have known that any call this far from home was trouble. She should have refused the kindly old woman who'd handed the receiver to her. *"Miss Mary."* Just by the way her name was said, she should have known. She never should have followed the directions. Never should have left the party. Never should have strayed from the house decorated with candy canes.

Darkness pressed on her. Her thoughts became fuzzy. She could sense that her hand was still reaching, still scratching though the snow, but she felt disconnected from her arm. Disconnected from the world. Deep in the darkness.

In the haze of snow and cold, her brain grasped at a sudden sensation, a smell that invaded her muddled thoughts. Peppermint. The spicy aroma surrounded her just as the snow did. The smell came from the necklace of mints she wore around her neck. A string of peppermints meant as a garland for the tree that, earlier in the evening, she had strung around herself instead. A festive gesture of a young, carefree girl. A girl full of life and promise.

She relaxed her frigid muscles. The smell seemed otherworldly. As if telling her that everything would be all right. That there would be justice. That someone would pay for her misery.

I will not be forgotten, she vowed.

CHAPTER 1

"They're not coming back," Ryan Garcia announced.

"What?" Kelly demanded. Gray slush from her boots fell in clumps onto the woven mat by the front door, leaving behind small pools of water. The warmth of the house felt good. The bus was like a freezer on wheels, and she was starving. Friday was Taco Day at school. So totally beyond disgusting, and of course, her mom hadn't packed her any lunch. For the last hour, she'd been thinking of nothing but the package of chocolate cookies waiting in the pantry.

"Mom and Dad," Ryan added.

Kelly kicked off her boots, and Ryan followed her across the front hall and into the kitchen. Her fuzzy blue socks slipped on the worn wooden floor. She dumped her backpack and hunter-green parka on one of the mismatched chairs, then turned to stare at her little brother. "What are you talking about?"

At ten years old, Ryan delighted in taunting her with secrets. His days were spent scheming to possess more information, as if it made him smarter or more grown-up. He still hadn't clued in: She didn't really care. Usually.

Ryan watched her open the pantry and grab the foil package. She slid out four cookies. They were the oversize, hockey-puck kind. *Four seems like the right number to make up for lunch,* Kelly reasoned. She ate the first one and let him wait. She knew he wanted her to ask again. To beg for more information. Ryan fidgeted, trying so hard not to tell her anything until she asked.

She ate the second cookie, chewing slowly. "So?" she finally said.

"So . . . we're all alone," Ryan reported. He looked unsure.

"Meaning?"

"Meaning Mom and Dad aren't coming back. Just like I told you."

Kelly studied her brother's face. He wasn't smiling or smirking. Had something bad really happened? Her mind raced through the possibilities. Car accident. Plane crash. She grabbed his arm. "Ryan, come on. Tell me what's going on."

"Snowstorm," Ryan said, swatting her hand off his sweatshirt. "They're staying in Philly."

Kelly took a deep breath, annoyed that her brother had almost scared her. It was only for a second, but still. *That's my job,* she thought. *Everyone knows that I'm the best at scaring people.*

"When did they call?" Kelly asked, biting into another cookie.

"About ten minutes ago." Ryan grabbed a cookie from the package too. The elementary school bus got home before her middle school bus. Mom and Dad must have called just as Ryan let himself into the house. "There's a blizzard or something. They're going to call back."

And just at that moment, the phone rang.

"Guess that's them." Kelly hurried to the phone on her mother's desk in the far corner of the kitchen. Her mom referred to her desk as "Command Central." In the middle sat a huge calendar with all their activities, and scattered about were school directories, recipes printed from the Internet, magazines she hadn't yet read, and a whole mess of other papers. Kelly never understood what gave her mother the right to be on her case about cleaning her room when her desk was such a disaster.

"Hi," Kelly said, sitting on the wooden desk chair.

"Kelly, honey, I'm so glad you're home," her mother panted. She sounded strangely out of breath.

"Of course I'm home. Got to get ready for my party. Lots to do," Kelly reminded her.

"Oh, Kels." Her mother sighed. "Listen, about that. Daddy and I are stuck in Philadelphia."

"Ryan told me." She glanced above the desk at the enormous bulletin board covered with articles and downloads. Her mom, among a million other things, wrote a column for their weekly town paper called It Happened Here. It was about all the unimportant things masquerading as history that had happened in their little Vermont town since the French trappers first arrived. Kelly kept telling her mom no one cared. But the editors kept asking for columns. She guessed it gave the newspaper a reason to exist, because there was certainly no real news going on in her town. The bulletin board was like a mini history lesson, if anyone cared to read the columns, which she didn't. Kelly usually just read the captions to the photos while she was on the phone.

"It's snowing like crazy here. They canceled all flights out of the airport." Her mom sounded tired. She'd been up since dawn.

"What are you going to do?"

"We thought about renting a car, but the weather report says the storm is heading up the East Coast. A big nor'easter. Should be in Vermont by nightfall. The roads will be a mess." Kelly could hear her dad in the background, trying to tell her mom something. "The only sensible thing for us to do is to spend the night in a hotel here."

"Oh. Okay." Kelly had never stayed alone in the house overnight. She felt fine with it, though. She had babysat for little kids down the street, and that was no big deal. She could totally handle Ryan. Between the TV and his video games, he'd stay out of her way. Besides, Paige and June were sleeping over tonight. An early birthday celebration. She'd have company.

"Daddy and I will leave first thing in the morning to get back home," her mom promised. Kelly could hear the worry in her voice. "What, Dave? How can they not have rooms? Look, the meeting wasn't my brilliant idea. It's fine . . . whatever . . . anywhere . . ." Her mom argued with her dad in the background. They had a company together, Authentic Vermont Blankets. Supposedly there was something about the sheep in their state that made superior wool for blankets—or at least, that was what her parents advertised. They had flown to Philadelphia this morning to try to convince some big store to sell their wool blankets instead of Amish quilts.

Kelly peered at a photocopy of a news clipping on the bulletin board about a woman named Mary Owens. She had never noticed this one before. The picture showed a young woman wearing a mod 1960s minidress and tall white patent-leather boots. A one-of-a-kind homemade necklace was draped about her neck. She sat serenely on a sofa, a playful smile on her thin lips. A Christmas tree decorated with candy canes filled the space behind her.

Her mom sighed. "Your dad could only find us a room in some ramshackle motel." Kelly could hear other voices and the muffled reverberations of loudspeaker announcements. She guessed they were still at the airport. "Kel, listen. I need you and Ryan to stay put. No going outside. And lock the doors."

"Sure." She studied the perfect swoosh of Mary's chestnut hair across her forehead. She wondered if her shoulder-length dark-brown hair could do that too. Doubtful.

"Chrissie is coming over at six," her mom continued. "She's bringing a pizza for dinner."

Kelly tore her gaze away from pretty Mary Owens. "Chrissie Cox? Why is she bringing us dinner?" Chrissie was her best friend Paige's older sister.

"Chrissie will be staying with you and Ryan tonight."

"A babysitter?" Kelly cried. "You got us a babysitter? I'm way too old for a babysitter! I'm in middle school."

"I know how old you are," her mother said. "But I'm not leaving you and your brother alone overnight. It's not safe. Plus, a big storm is coming."

"But Mom, we won't be alone," Kelly reminded her. "Paige and June are coming for the sleepover."

"Kelly, that can't happen tonight. Not without me or your dad there."

"That's not fair! It's not my fault there's a storm. It's my birthday!" Kelly cried.

"No, it's not," Ryan piped in behind her.

She shot him an evil glare. He crossed his eyes at her. "Real mature," Kelly muttered.

"We'll move your birthday celebration to next

weekend," her mother said. "Besides, your birthday is really on Tuesday," she rationalized, as if Kelly didn't know when it was. "So next Friday will work just as well."

Kelly groaned. Typical of her mother. She always moved holidays to suit her own schedule. They often had Thanksgiving on a Sunday so her mother's whole family could drive in, and Easter on a Saturday so they didn't have to fight the weekend traffic home from Boston.

"But—" She had planned so many great things for tonight.

"No buts, Kelly. I'm counting on you. I'll call back later," her mom said. "Dad and I need to find this motel before the roads become impassable."

"Okay." She sighed. She wasn't happy, but she didn't have a choice. She knew that. No sleepover. She passed the phone to Ryan. As he babbled about some science project in school with pennies and sugar water, Kelly took a closer look at Mary Owens. The caption under the picture said the photo had been snapped at a Christmas party right before her untimely death.

Kelly stood on the chair and unpinned the article. She began reading from the beginning. All the while, she had the strangest feeling that the gaze of the young woman in the picture was fixed on her. Wanting her to know what had happened. Mary's story was so tragic. Killed in a freak avalanche. Suffocated under the weight of the snow.

Staring into her soulful eyes, Kelly wondered what it felt like, alone, buried under all that whiteness.

"Mom said we should watch the Weather Channel." Ryan had hung up the phone and was standing over her. "What's that?"

"One of Mom's articles. Scary stuff." She pinned it back onto the bulletin board before he could reach for it. "I'm going to my room." She glanced out the window over the sink. The sky remained its usual winter gray. Thick clouds but no storm.

All this craziness over nothing, she thought. *I've been look-ing forward to this sleepover all week, and now I have to sit here with a babysitter, totally bored.*

She had no idea of the horrors that lay ahead.

CHAPTER 2

Kelly made her way up the stairs, the floorboards of their renovated farmhouse creaking under her weight. Her bedroom was down the hall to the right. A vision in pink and green.

She'd begged her parents all year to let her redecorate, but her mom refused. She couldn't accept that Kelly had long since outgrown the plaid decor she had picked out when Kelly was still crawling. Kelly had the feeling she'd be living in preppy paradise until she left for college.

She tossed her book bag on the carnation-pink carpet, next to the rolled-up pair of jeans she'd tried on, then rejected, this morning. Pulling out the white chair that matched her desk set, she booted up her laptop, then quickly IMed Paige and June.

Kookykell2011: Hi. Bad news.

Juney206: ?

Kookykell2011: No sleepover tonight. Parents trapped in snow in Philly.

Paige4peace421: I heard. Can't believe your mom thinks Chrissie is gonna keep u safe! LOL

Kookykell2011: Spare me. So not my idea!

Juney206: U have a babysitter!!!???!! Chrissie!

Kookykell2011: Not my idea!!!!

Paige4peace421: It is kinda scary at night alone . . .

Juney206: Ooooooh! Better watch out!

Kookykell2011: So NOT scared!

Juney206: What about your sleepover?

Paige4peace421: Yeah. I have a present 4 u.

Juney206: Me 2.

Kookykell2011: Thx. U guys r the best. I have to move it to next weekend. Stinks. Had so many great scares planned for u tonight!

Paige4peace421: Maybe I'm safer at home! Ha ha!

A sudden, terrified shriek filled the house.

Ryan pounded up the stairs, taking them two at a time. "Kelly!" he cried. He burst into her room.

"What's wrong?" she asked, pushing back in her chair to see him.

"Look what I found." He gingerly held up what appeared to be a severed finger wrapped in a napkin.

"Ooh, gross." She shrank back. She could see all the tiny wrinkles in the skin and the nail still in place on the end. So alive. So real.

"Don't act all innocent," he said. "I know it was you."

"What are you talking about?" she asked. "Are you okay?"

Ryan sneered. "Like you care."

Kelly raised her eyebrows in confusion.

"I know you're the one who stuck this fake finger in the cookie package." Ryan's face reddened in anger.

"It's scary when kids get too greedy. Got to keep your fingers out of the cookie jar, as some people say." Kelly couldn't hide her triumphant grin. Ryan was such an easy target for a scare. There really was no sport in it. He fell for her frights every time. After all these years, she would've thought he'd wise up. But she was glad he stayed so gullible. She loved hearing his frightened cries.

"Ha-ha." He turned to leave. "I'm watching TV. Leave me alone tonight."

"Gladly," she replied, swiveling back to her screen.

SpenceX77: HEY.
Kookykell2011: HEY.

Spencer Stone logged onto their chat session. Kelly filled him in on the blizzard situation. He lived across the street from Kelly, and Paige lived behind her house. June Prendergast was only around the block. The four had been friends since tricycle days. There was a goofy photo of them all squeezed into a red wagon around age three in a frame on her desk.

Kelly's cell buzzed, and she wiggled her shiny blue phone out of her jeans pocket. There was a voice mail. *This phone has the worst service,* she thought. As Paige and June greeted Spencer, she listened to the long message from her mom. They had arrived at the motel, and her mom wasn't happy. *That makes two of us,* Kelly thought. *She's not getting any sympathy from me.* Then she grinned. Her mother's story gave her an idea. She instantly knew how to add lots of spooky touches to really freak out her friends. A classic Kelly scare. Her fingers flew over the keyboard.

Kookykell2011: YOU GUYS WON'T BELIEVE WHAT JUST HAPPENED TO MY PARENTS. THE TAXI LET THEM OFF IN FRONT

OF A RUN-DOWN BUILDING ON THE FAR EDGE OF PHILLY. THE
ENTIRE STREET WAS BLANKETED IN DRIFTS OF SNOW. EVEN IN
THE STORM, MY MOM COULD SEE THIS WAS THE KIND OF PLACE
YOU ONLY CHECKED INTO IF YOU WERE DESPERATE, WHICH
THEY WERE. THE BRICKS WERE CRACKED, THICK DUST LINED
THE WINDOWS, AND THE ROOF SLUMPED IN AT A DANGEROUS
ANGLE. THE TAXI PULLED AWAY, DISAPPEARING DOWN THE
STREET, LEAVING THEM ALONE. EVERYTHING WAS COMPLETELY
SILENT. THERE WERE NO OTHER CARS. NO SOUNDS. NOTHING.

Juney206: OMG! DID THEY GO IN?

Paige4peace421: I WOULDN'T.

Kookykell2011: THEY HAD NO CHOICE. THEY PUSHED
OPEN THE HEAVY WOODEN DOOR AND STEPPED INTO COMPLETE
BLACKNESS. NO LIGHTS. THEY CALLED OUT BUT GOT NO ANSWER.
MY FATHER REACHED AROUND DESPERATELY FOR A LIGHT
SWITCH. SOON HIS FINGERS FELT ONE, AND HE FLICKED IT ON
AND . . . BEHIND THE FRONT DESK SAT A SKELETON. WHO
KNEW HOW LONG THE BODY HAD BEEN THERE, ROTTING AWAY?
THE FLESH HAD DECOMPOSED AND ONLY THE BONES REMAINED
. . . SITTING THERE, WAITING TO GREET THE GUESTS. THEN THE
MOTEL PHONE RANG. IT RANG AND RANG. MY FATHER TOOK
A HESITANT STEP FORWARD AND LIFTED THE RECEIVER. HELLO?
HE SAID.

SpenceX77: WHO WAS CALLING? WHAT DID THEY SAY?????

Kookykell2011: HE SAID GOTCHA! KELLY RULES!

She laughed as her friends typed back, annoyed that she had done it again.

Kookykell2011: I AM THE QUEEN OF SCARES!

She'd been scaring her friends for years. In elementary school, she was mostly about fake snakes and eyeballs. And while those were still awesome, especially when skillfully placed in a lunch bag, she'd moved on in middle school to creepy stories about monsters and creatures and ghosts. The real spine-tingling stuff. Everyone agreed that she was the master.

Kelly glanced around her empty room, suddenly feeling a bit let down. A scary story wasn't the same when she couldn't see her friends' reactions. That was the whole adrenaline rush. The look of pure fear. She couldn't get that typing on a screen. *This no-sleepover thing stinks,* she thought. Everything was ready. Her green flannel sleeping bag was rolled out on her floor, with a plastic bag of scares tucked underneath. A fake fuzzy mouse to slip under June's pillow. A book of ghost stories. A tiny, handheld device that emitted bloodcurdling screams and vicious growls. *It would have been perfect,* Kelly thought. She didn't want to wait until next week.

That was when she had a brilliant idea.

Kookykell2011: LET'S HAVE A WEBCAM SLEEPOVER TONIGHT. ALL OF US.

SpenceX77: WHAT'S THAT?

Kookykell2011: JUST LIKE A REAL ONE BUT VIRTUAL. WE ALL PUT ON OUR WEBCAMS SO WE CAN SEE EACH OTHER AND JUST HANG LIKE WE WOULD IF WE WERE TOGETHER. EXCEPT WITH THE COMPUTER. SPENCER CAN HANG TOO.

SpenceX77: EXCELLENT! NEVER BEEN TO A GIRLS' SLEEPOVER.

Kookykell2011: EIGHT O'CLOCK! WEAR PJ'S!

Paige4peace421: AWESOME!

Juney206: C U THEN.

Kookykell2011: BEFORE YOU GUYS GO, I HAVE TO WARN YOU ABOUT SOMETHING.

Paige4peace421: WHAT?

Kookykell2011: IT'S SERIOUS.

SpenceX77: SPIT IT OUT.

Kookykell2011: GET READY TO BE SCARED! VERY SCARED!

CHAPTER 3

Kelly opened the front door that evening for Chrissie and immediately shivered at the drop in temperature. The air had plummeted to way below freezing, causing the snow of the past week to crust over into a shiny shell. Chrissie, pizza box in hand, slid a bit on the front walk. Her blond hair poked out of a knit cap, and a puffy navy parka swallowed up her thin body.

Glancing out into the early evening darkness, Kelly still didn't see her mother's big storm approaching. Just the same heavy gray clouds, the Stones' SUV pulling into their driveway across the street, and Mr. Golubic, wrapped in a thick wool coat, walking his black Labrador, weaving around the snowdrifts on the side of the road. The usual New England winter stuff.

A little before eight, Kelly stood up from the over-stuffed family room sofa, where Ryan and Chrissie were watching reality-show reruns.

"Time for the webcam sleepover?" Chrissie asked. She smiled knowingly.

"Paige told you?" Paige and Chrissie had this weird relationship. Sometimes they were the best of friends, and sometimes Chrissie went into superior-older-sister mode, acting as if Paige were an alien life form best to be avoided. The hard thing, for an outsider like Kelly, was figuring out which dynamic was playing out when.

"Yeah. Sounds like fun." Chrissie smiled, crinkling her blue eyes the same way Paige did.

Kelly had to admit that Chrissie was probably the best choice if she was forced to have a babysitter, which obviously she was. A senior in high school, Chrissie starred in all the school plays but wasn't a drama queen. She was actually pretty laid-back, and she seemed more into talking on her phone than the whole babysitter authority thing. She was fine with letting Ryan and Kelly do what they wanted, which worked for Kelly.

Chrissie's ringtone trilled an upbeat tune from a current Broadway musical. "Just come downstairs every once in a while, so I know you're still breathing," Chrissie said before she walked away to answer her phone.

Kelly closed her bedroom door and changed into striped flannel pajama pants and a long-sleeved sweatshirt with polka dots. She nudged Ezra off her desk chair. The ten-year-old black cat stared at her, then scampered along the windowsill to the top of her dresser. He was her dad's cat. She wasn't exactly sure what his problem was, but the cat refused to live on ground level. He'd climb to the highest point in any room so he could reign supreme, staring haughtily down at the humans below.

Kelly pulled her hair into a ponytail, then switched on her webcam and logged into the conferencing site. Paige's face peered out from the top box on Kelly's screen. As perky as ever, she bounced up and down on her bed. Paige always bounced. On the bus. In the cafeteria. During class. Paige's mom called it nervous energy. Kelly glanced enviously at Paige flopping on her new teal-and-gray bedspread. Totally sophisticated.

Kelly waved into her webcam.

"How's Chrissie?" Paige asked. "Did she play games with you? Is she going to tuck you in?"

Kelly screwed up her face. "Ha-ha. Very funny."

"I think it's so cute that Kelly has a babysitter," June cooed.

Kelly gazed at a second box on her screen that framed June's face. Forever the glamour girl, she wore pink satin button-down men's-cut pajamas. Kelly doubted June owned a pair of sweats, and if she did, they were probably the velour kind, jeweled with rhinestones. June held two fingernails up to the camera. One was polished in iridescent purple; the other in a matte baby blue.

"Color choice?" she inquired.

Paige and Kelly both chose the sparkly purple. Kelly watched June, sitting at her vanity, her laptop certainly nestled among bottles of perfume and tubes of lip gloss, meticulously polishing her nails. Her long auburn hair fell like a curtain over her face as she bent in concentration.

"Should we all polish our nails?" Paige asked.

"Or we can make beauty masks," Kelly suggested. "I read that if you mix avocado with honey and smear it on your face it makes your skin glow."

"You serving chips with that?" Spencer's voice broke through as he appeared in a third box on her screen. "I mean, seriously, we're not really going to sit here and watch you girls have some sort of spa session, are we?"

"You would look good in a green face mask," Paige quipped. "Might mellow out all those freckles."

"Whoa! Back off the freckles," Spencer warned. "You only dream of having this much character on your face."

Paige laughed. "Just joking."

"So what's the plan?" asked a voice from behind Spencer.

"Who's that?" Kelly spotted a silhouette hovering behind Spencer, just out of view of the camera.

"Show yourself," June commanded.

"You guess," said the voice.

"Well, from your voice I can tell you're a guy." June giggled. Kelly rolled her eyes. June had recently started using this fake flirting giggle. Didn't she know it was so transparent?

"Do you go to our school?" Paige asked, leaning into her camera to catch a closer glimpse.

"Yes," the voice replied. Spencer sat at his desk, his secretive grin broadcasting to all their screens.

"Are you in any of our classes?" June asked.

"Kelly's," he said. "Math."

Kelly quickly did a mental scan of her math classroom.

Who was Spencer friends with in that class? Everyone she thought of, she rejected. She couldn't think of anyone that Spencer would hang with. She threw out a few random names, but the voice said she was wrong, wrong, and wrong.

"I give up," she admitted. "You win. Who are you?"

"The mystery person is . . ." Spencer used his game-show-announcer voice. He moved away from the camera, and for a moment, all that was visible was the *Avatar* poster on his bedroom wall. Then a face filled the screen.

Kelly gasped.

His eyes were crossed and his upper lip curled back, exposing an expanse of gums and huge upper teeth. Gruesome!

She needed a few moments to recognize Gavin Mahon. He was new to their school. He sat in the back corner of their math class. She had never spoken to him. She wondered how Spencer even knew him—and why he was hanging out at his house.

Spencer squeezed back into the screen next to Gavin, who had now uncontorted his face, and introduced him to June and Paige. While they were comparing classes and saying hi, Kelly took a closer look at Gavin. He was so unlike tall, sturdy Spencer. Gavin seemed younger and skinnier than other boys their age. His arms were thin and his neck was wiry. He wore his black hair in a bowl cut, and she could make out a faint scar above his thick eyebrows.

"Gavin started Adventure Guides with me," Spencer was saying when Kelly tuned back into the conversation. *That explains it,* she thought. Spencer was into nature, hiking, and fishing. Adventure Guides was some sort of survivalist group. Of course, skinny Gavin looked like the last person to rough it in the outdoors. "He's sleeping over tonight. A *real* sleepover."

"This one is real too," Paige protested. "And you guys should be in pj's if you want to participate." She scowled at their jeans and T-shirts.

Kelly was going to agree, when she heard a knock at her door. "Come in," she called.

Chrissie pushed open the door and pranced in, a bowl of mint chocolate chip ice cream in her hand. "Hello, sleepover people," she chirped. "I brought a yummy bowl of ice cream. Your favorite flavor, right, Paigey-o? Sleepovers should have treats . . . oh, but, wait"—she poked her head in front of the webcam—"you're not here to share it, are you Paigey-o? And I know there's no ice cream at our house. So sad for you."

Paige jumped up from her bed. "Get lost, Chrissie!" she yelled to the screen.

Chrissie continued to taunt her little sister. Kelly couldn't believe her mom was actually paying Chrissie. *I act more mature than she does,* she thought. Moving away from her desk, she let Chrissie slide into her chair. She stood alongside, watching Chrissie chat with her friends.

Suddenly Kelly sucked in her breath. "Oh, man. Chrissie, don't move. Seriously. Don't."

"W-what? What's happening?" Chrissie asked, her voice shaking.

Kelly tried to scream, but no sound came out. All she could do was point at the bare skin on Chrissie's neck. It was horrible. So horrible.

Chrissie stiffened. "Please. Tell me!"

"It's on you," Kelly whispered. She inched backward. "Oh, watch out! It's going to bite."

CHAPTER 4

"A spider." Kelly gulped. "There's a huge spider on you."

Chrissie jerked her head, trying without success to see the spider. Her cheeks flamed, and her scream rose throughout the house. Ezra arched his back in protest. Leaping from the dresser onto the desk, he shot out the door in a black flash of fur, raising the pitch of Chrissie's scream an octave.

"Get it off!" she wailed.

"I don't know. . . ." Kelly stared at the enormous black spider. "It's so . . . so hairy!"

"Help me! It's going to bite. I know it!"

Kelly took a deep breath. She reached over and, with the back of her hand, knocked the spider from Chrissie's neck. She froze as it landed on Chrissie's sneaker.

Chrissie shrieked again. "Are you crazy?"

"Gotcha!" Kelly cried. "Smile for the cameras!" All her friends laughed, as she waved the fake tarantula in Chrissie's face. Paige danced on her bed, delighted that her big sister had fallen for the lamest scare ever.

Chrissie scowled. "Ooh, that was bad. You freaked me out."

Kelly shrugged. "I am the master. With me, you should always be ready for a scare."

"Who's there? Hey, Kelly! Hi! Hi, June! Can you see me?" Spencer's six-year-old brother Charlie's gap-toothed grin filled the screen.

Charlie is way cute, Kelly thought. They'd all been friends since long before he was born, and Charlie kind of felt like a younger brother to her, too.

"Get lost," Spencer said, playfully pushing Charlie out of the way. "Aren't you supposed to be going to bed?"

"Take a hike, squirt," Gavin added. Kelly detected a slight edge in his voice. As if he didn't like Charlie.

"You're mean." Charlie's whine could be heard.

"Yeah," June agreed. "Be nice."

"Charlie, sweetie, leave your brother alone." Spencer's mom's voice sounded faint, as if she was down the hall.

The ringtone of Chrissie's phone filled the room. "Ugh, I hate that song," Paige said, leaning back against her oversize pillows and pulling out her own phone to check messages.

"I kind of like it." June stood and shimmied to the beat. "It's got a good groove."

"Not when you hear the same show tune every two minutes," Paige complained. "Chrissie's obsessed with Broadway musicals."

Chrissie glanced at the caller ID, then let the call go to voice mail. "Okay, I'm done here. I'll be downstairs watching TV with Ryan—" The Broadway hit trilled again. Chrissie screwed up her face. "Nobody has any patience. I gotta get this."

Kelly heard Chrissie talking into the phone as she padded down the stairs. Kelly plopped back onto her chair and kicked her feet up onto the desk. "What we need," she announced, "is a ghost story."

"Ooh, good idea," Paige said. "Everyone turn off the lights."

"Mood lighting," June agreed.

As she stood to reach for the light switch, Kelly glanced out the small window between her desk and her dresser.

Through the overgrown tangle of tree branches, frosted white from storms earlier in the week, she could make out the first flurries slowly falling. The storm was starting.

"Kel, don't you have a big book of ghost stories?" Spencer asked, his face lit by the greenish glow of his monitor, the room behind him completely dark.

Kelly nodded and was about to reach for it when Gavin said, "I know a story."

All eyes turned to him.

"It's a true story, though. Is that okay?" He sat on a chair next to Spencer, so the camera aimed on both their faces.

"True is better," June said, purple light surrounding her as if part of a surreal music video. June must have her bedside lamp on. The one with the purple bulb.

"What's it about?" Paige asked.

"You need some background," Gavin began. "I come from a small town in the way northern part of the state, right near the Canadian border. It isn't really a town. More like a bunch of cabins in the woods. My dad worked for a lumber mill."

He blinked several times. "Things were different up there. People weren't so friendly. Or so trusting. We pretty much kept to ourselves. Except for one night every year."

Kelly leaned closer, studying Gavin's face. It had an intensity she had never seen before.

"Every year, on January twenty-ninth, we'd gather at the old Richardson place. It wasn't that we much liked the company. It was just accepted that on a night like that, there was safety in numbers." He pushed his fingertips together, methodically cracking each knuckle. "The howling started at nightfall."

"What howling?" Spencer asked.

"Animals. The attacks started small. Rabbits and squirrels. Then bigger animals. Foxes. Deer." Gavin swallowed hard. "The cries would then grow louder, more intense. The shrieks of geese. The wails of wolves."

"Why were they making all that noise?" Paige wrapped her arms around a pillow, hugging it close.

Gavin blinked rapidly. A nervous habit? "Death is painful. Vicious. Especially under the powerful grip of the Lagad."

"The what?" Was Gavin making this up? Normally Kelly would have thought so. But that cold, faraway look in his eyes was the stare of someone who had witnessed horrible things.

"The people who were natives to the woods called it—him—the Lagad. An ancient name."

"What was it?" Paige wanted to know.

Gavin paused. "Hard to tell. Some said it was a man who had turned into a hairy, ravenous creature. Some said it was a huge creature that had humanlike traits. Whatever it was, it was supernatural and deadly. It descended from the mountains on this one night every year as an act of revenge against the loggers who had destroyed its lair on that very day generations ago. The Lagad returned to settle the score."

"By killing animals?"

"It warmed up with animals," he explained. "As the hour grew later, it tracked people. The same way some people hunt deer . . . silently following tracks . . . scents. Alone in your house, you were no match for the Lagad. You would hear the crunch of its footsteps, maybe the crack of a twig, the scraping of its claws against your door, and then it was all over."

"Did you ever see it?" June asked.

His right eyelid twitched involuntarily as he measured his response. "Yes."

Kelly could hear herself breathing. Had the creature done something that had caused Gavin to leave his home? To move down here?

Gavin stared into the distance, remembering that terrible time. "My brother and I were home alone. We should've been at Richardson's place, keeping the vigil with everyone else. But we were waiting for my dad. His truck had broken down, and he was coming from the mechanic. To get us. It was too long a walk in the cold to Richardson's, so we waited. We waited too long."

Kelly pulled her sweatshirt sleeves over her hands. The darkness of the room cocooned her, transporting her to that desolate cabin in the northern woods.

"We were upstairs when we heard the noises at the back door. Grunts. Pounding. We huddled together. Terrified. It was here. It was coming for us. There was nowhere to hide. And then we heard the splintering of wood. . . ."

Kelly could hear the scraping of the creature's claws. The cracking of the door as the creature banged its way into the cabin. So close. Scraping, scraping.

She let out a low moan as the sound grew louder. The creature was coming.

Suddenly she knew. The scraping wasn't part of Gavin's story. She could hear the sound. In her room. Behind her.

Something was trying to get in. Something was trying to get her!

She whirled around.

Nothing.

She scanned the darkness. Her monitor threw off enough light to make out the outlines of her bed, night table, and dresser. Gavin continued to speak, but she tuned him out. Slowly she stood. Her legs trembled as the scraping came again.

From the window.

Her hands freezing with fear, she edged away from the desk and stepped silently toward the window.

CHAPTER 5

Kelly gazed though the window and jumped back. Bare branches slapped at the glass.

She shook her head at her own stupidity. How could she have gotten so sucked in by Gavin's story? It was just the wind causing the trees to scrape the windowpane. No one was there.

"Kelly? What happened? You okay?" Paige called out.

She was glad she was out of view. *I'm supposed to be the one doing the scaring,* she chided herself. *Not the one being scared. Such an amateur move.* From now on, she'd take control of the sleepover—at least, the scaring part.

She pulled the cord, closing her shade to the movements of the night. "Just checking on the storm," she called back. "Wind's picking up." She returned to her position in front of her webcam as if she'd merely taken a casual stroll across her room. She'd missed the end of Gavin's story. She wondered what happened, although now, by the grins on her friends' faces, she suspected he'd been making it all up. Figured.

"I have an idea." Paige leaned toward the monitor. "We should summon the dead."

"I like it." June nodded with a mischievous glint in her eyes. "Who should we bring back?"

"John Lennon?" Spencer suggested.

Gavin elbowed him. "Oh yeah, he's a real scary music dude."

"How about Cleopatra?" June said. "She had the coolest jewelry."

"No way," Gavin retorted. "A mummy would be creepy. Not a queen."

"I think we need someone we have a connection to. You know, to make it mean something," Paige said. "Someone from around here. Maybe someone who died a long time ago in a strange way or—"

"Guys!" Kelly interrupted. "I have the perfect person." She closed her eyes, bringing forth the pretty face in her mind. The clear, innocent gaze. She'd never been one to believe in fate and all that. She was a straightforward facts kind of girl. But this felt as if it was meant to be. As if there was a true connection. "We will call forth the spirit of Miss Mary Owens."

"Who?" all her friends wanted to know.

"I'll tell you about Mary." She paused as the old heater in the attic above her clanked, revving up to fight the cold creeping through the ancient wood siding. The wind gusted, and the branches rattled against the house. "She died on a night like this."

"How do you know about her?" Paige asked.

Kelly told them about the article she'd read that afternoon. "The year was 1966. Mary was young, like Chrissie's age. She'd come to our town to visit her aunt for the holidays. Her aunt lived out past the MacMaster farm, near the base of the big mountain. Back then there were no strip malls. Just houses and farms. And in Vermont, in the winter, there was snow. Lots and lots of it."

She paused to recollect the story. "Her aunt threw a large party. Lots of people. Caroling and food and holiday cheer. Mary had an eye for beauty. She decorated her aunt's tree with dozens of candy canes. She wove garlands with those round red-and-white peppermint candies and strung them throughout the rooms. Guests remarked on the scent of peppermint that filled the house. Mary even placed mints on a string and wore it as a necklace, surrounding herself with the holiday aroma.

"Now, crafty is nice where grown-ups are concerned, but Mary was beautiful, too. So, of course, the local boys at the party noticed her. And, of course, the local girls noticed the local boys noticing Mary, which didn't go over so well. Especially when some of those boys were the boyfriends of some of those jealous girls."

Kelly pictured Mary sitting by the fireplace, in her red-and-white dress, laughing lightly as a group of boys brought her punch and iced gingerbread cookies. Good for Mary. Not so good for the ignored girlfriends.

"During the party, the phone rang. The caller asked for *Miss Mary*. Mary took the call in the privacy of the kitchen, but she didn't go back to the party. No one noticed it at the time. She immediately went out the back door, wearing only her party dress. Snow had started to fall, and more was on its way. No one would ever know who called or what the caller had said. But something drove Mary to walk through the snow, without a coat, to the shed at the farthest part of the property in the darkness of a freezing winter night."

"What happened then?" Spencer asked.

"Before this, there had been days and days of storms. Wet, heavy snow was piled everywhere. A huge mound of snow and ice had accumulated on the shed roof. Mary entered the rickety shed alone. Why? Who knows. The door must've slammed behind her, setting off an avalanche of the snow on the roof. The rumbling was deafening. There was no time to run. Nowhere to go. Tons of snow crashed in a wave as the roof crumbled.

"Mary was found the next morning. The article said the smell of mint filled the destroyed cabin. She had tried to claw her way out of the suffocating whiteness, and her bare hands were frozen in place. Her mouth was forever stuck in a horrified scream. She had been buried alive."

The faint whirring of her computer was the only sound Kelly could hear. Her friends remained silent, their thoughts with the helpless girl.

Kelly continued. "Some of the girls from the party were suspected of luring her out there. But no one could prove anything. It could have been anyone. A secret past, perhaps? And no one could have known that all that heavy snow would have thundered down. The case is still unsolved." She took a deep breath and stared straight into the camera. "People say that Mary's spirit hasn't left the area. They say that she wanders about on the snowiest nights. They say that she strikes out at the young, trying to take their life the way her life was taken tragically early."

"I say we find Mary." June's eyes widened with excitement.

"Definitely," Paige agreed.

"But how?" Spencer asked.

Kelly waited for Gavin to say something, but he remained silent. She took this as agreement. "Here's what we do."

She frowned at Paige. Sprawled on her bed, her friend's fingers tap-danced across her phone. Paige was an obsessive texter. "Put down the phone. Put down everything. Full concentration is needed."

Paige rolled her eyes, finished her text, and rested her cell on her night table.

Only the dim, greenish glow from the monitors illuminated each room, casting sickly shadows on the friends' faces.

Kelly recalled all she knew about summoning spirits

of the dead. "Next we each need a reflective surface."

"What about our screens? I can sort of see myself in mine," Spencer said.

"That should work," Gavin said. His face appeared strangely pale. Bad lighting for them all.

"Okay, to call back Miss Mary, each of us must chant her name thirteen times as we spin in a circle. One chant per turn, our voices growing louder, drawing her to us. On the thirteenth time, stop spinning and stare at the reflective surface." Kelly surreptitiously placed the little scream machine out of sight on the edge of her desk. Her plan was to press the button and sound the bloodcurdling scream at just the right moment to freak out her friends.

"Clear your minds," Gavin instructed solemnly, as if he'd done this before. "Think only of poor Mary. Trapped in the snow. Alone. Focus on her tortured soul."

Kelly bit her lip in anticipation as they began. Standing in the darkness, she slowly turned in a circle. "Miss Mary."

"Miss Mary."

"Miss Mary."

Around and around they spun. Some standing, some sitting on revolving desk chairs.

"Miss Mary. Miss Mary." Their voices rose, calling the name of the dead girl. The eerie green glow was the only beacon in a spinning whirl of darkness.

"Miss Mary. Miss Mary."

Kelly was losing count. Losing balance. The face of Miss Mary swam before her eyes. Drowning in an avalanche of green light. Pulling her under. Down, down. Around.

"Miss Mary." Calling for her. "Miss Mary!"

Louder, louder, their voices crying out in unison. Reaching beyond the years. Reaching into the depths. The air crackled around them. An electric current sent jolts throughout her body.

The final dizzy turn.

The screech of her name ripped from their throats.

And then the gasps. Kelly blinked, disoriented, hearing everyone gasp. Desperately she tried to focus on her monitor. She was dizzy. Oh, so dizzy.

"Kelly!" June's face froze in wide-eyed horror. "S-she's behind you!"

CHAPTER 6

Swallowing hard, Kelly peered over her shoulder. Darkness greeted her. Her eyes roamed the room. Silhouettes of stuffed animals on her bed. The lump of her school bag on the floor.

No one.

She sank into her chair, pulling her monitor close. Her heart beat fast. "Who? Who did you see? There's no one here." She glanced again to be sure.

Shadows. The rush of the wind.

"She was there. Behind you." June trembled.

"I saw her too," Paige said. "For a second, she appeared on your screen. Then she was gone."

"That was so weird," Spencer murmured.

"Who? What did she look like?" Kelly wavered. Were

her friends tricking her? She wanted to believe so, but their faces told her otherwise. They had seen something.

"More of a shadow than an actual person," Paige murmured.

"But it was definitely a woman," June added. "I could see her silhouette. Hovering there. Just for a second. Oh, wow, Kel, she was totally in your room."

A chill ran down Kelly's spine. She hugged her arms around her chest, trying to make sense of it all. "Do you think it worked? Do you think we really brought her back?"

No one wanted to speak first. To say the thing they all felt, yet couldn't explain.

"I saw it . . . her . . . too." Gavin broke the silence. "The last time we said Mary's name. She was there. She was real."

"Awesome!" Spencer's spark returned. "We did it. We brought back the dead."

"I think it's creepy," Paige said. "Don't you, Kelly? I mean, she was in your room."

Kelly reached over and ran her fingers along the tiny black plastic box on her desk. She'd never pressed the button and sounded the scream. She'd never had the chance to pretend the supernatural could be contacted, because . . . it might have really happened. She shifted her weight in her chair. She was unsure of what she felt. She wished she had seen what they'd seen. "Let's do it again."

"What?" June sat straighter.

She shrugged. "To be sure. Let's see if it's really her. Do it all again. The chanting. All of it." She tucked a stray piece of hair behind her ear, suddenly excited by the idea.

"Sure." Spencer was up for anything.

"It was freaky, but okay." Paige was in.

"No way." Gavin nudged Spencer into the shadows, making sure Kelly could see him on her monitor. His beady eyes bored into the screen. His face remained grim. "You don't mess with the dead."

"Oh, please!" Paige snorted, no longer scared. "Let's do it."

"I'm serious. Once was enough." Gavin blinked quickly many times. "Trust me."

"Why? What makes you an expert?" Kelly wanted to know.

He cast his eyes downward for a moment, still blinking nervously. "Nothing." He paused, cracking one knuckle, then another. "You made contact. You've started things in motion—"

"What things?" she demanded.

Gavin shrugged. "Things we don't understand. Things from beyond. Things that should be left alone."

He's so weird, Kelly decided. She thought of texting Paige and seeing if she thought so too. It didn't feel natural to have him here with them. What right did he have to dictate what they could do?

"Well, I—" She stopped, suddenly hearing a faint melody. The notes repeated. An unsettling tune.

"You know," June began hesitantly, "I sort of agree with Gavin. I don't think we should do it again."

"Really?" Kelly asked. She was surprised. June usually liked adventure.

"I felt something," June whispered. She looked embarrassed.

"What?" Kelly and Paige asked in unison.

June gnawed a hangnail on her thumb. "Didn't you? A tingling kind of thing? Right before she appeared?" She gazed at them hopefully.

Kelly hesitated. Had she felt something? She wasn't sure. Maybe . . . maybe some static electricity. But did ghosts give off that kind of energy? And sure, she was dizzy, but that could've just been from the spinning.

"I felt it," Gavin replied.

Paige shrugged. So did Spencer.

Kelly shook her head. "No way. It's all in our heads. Come on. One more time." Suddenly, for some unexplained reason, she wanted to show her friends that it had just been a weird group hallucination. That it couldn't be true. She would do something the next time that would scare them—the fake growl, perhaps—and then they would know it wasn't real and—

The melody sounded again. Louder this time.

The same eight sinister notes. A haunting tune.

"What's that song?" Paige asked. "Kel, did you put music on?"

"No."

Everyone listened as the tune repeated twice more. So loud. As if right outside her door.

"Probably something Ryan is watching," Kelly guessed. "I'm going to check. Be right back. Don't do anything without me, okay?"

She walked across her room and rested her hand on the door handle. Straining her ears, she listened for the melody. The low buzz of garbled TV voices was the only noise she could make out from downstairs. The music had stopped. She pushed open her door and poked her head into the darkened hallway.

The smell immediately overwhelmed her.

Inhaling, she felt weightless, spiraling back in time. To a farmhouse in the snow. To a party filled with cheer . . . and despair. The scent surrounded her. Made her dizzy. She grasped the door handle to anchor herself.

She drew her breath in again, just be sure. The smell was undeniable. Peppermint.

The icy mint aroma filled her nostrils. And she knew: *Miss Mary is here.*

CHAPTER 7

She froze in the doorway, unsure of where to go or what to do. Her eyes darted about the hallway and over her shoulder, into her room. She had no idea what to look for. Her heart beat rapidly.

Peppermint. She smelled peppermint.

Would a ghost leave behind an odor? she wondered. Did it mean Mary's spirit was here? Now?

She wanted to run to her computer and tell her friends about the peppermint smell. She could hear the murmuring of their voices coming from her computer speakers. June's high-pitched giggle. The lower tone of Gavin. A sudden overwhelming wave of logic and disbelief prevented her from turning back.

She shook her head, trying to straighten out her

thoughts. *Get a grip. There is no ghost,* she reminded herself. *I told the story from the newspaper to scare everyone else. Not to scare myself.*

She inhaled again. The crisp scent of mint wafted around her.

Then it hit her. *Chrissie must be baking something with peppermint in it,* she thought. *Maybe chocolate mint cookies or hot chocolate with peppermint oil.*

Much relieved, Kelly padded down the stairs in her fuzzy socks. She stopped midway, her hand resting on the oak banister. Drawing in another breath, she noticed that the peppermint was no longer as overpowering. The farther down the stairs she moved, the more the scent weakened. At the bottom, it was almost nonexistent.

She glanced out the front window, watching as the wind swirled the flurries in crazy circles. Under the glow of the streetlamps, the snow appeared as a magical coating decorating the walkway. It reminded her of the silver glitter she used to pour onto school projects. Mounds of shiny flecks piled on gobs of white glue.

She turned toward the back of the house. To her left, she could hear the TV in the family room. Two men arguing on the screen. She continued into the kitchen, expecting to see Chrissie by the oven or stove.

"Whatcha baking?" Kelly called out.

She was met with silence. The lights were on, but the kitchen was empty.

She could detect the slight smell of the pepperoni from tonight's pizza. No peppermint. No aroma even vaguely like peppermint.

The large chrome stove and double oven on the far left wall of the farm-style kitchen was dark and cold. Nothing cooking. The granite counter on the center island held only today's mail and a pizza box with uneaten crusts. Her mother's desk on the far right wall appeared to be in the same state of disorganization as earlier. The door to the basement at the right of the desk remained firmly shut. Even though her parents had bought sofas, a Ping-Pong table, and a foosball table to make it into a "playroom," she and Ryan rarely went down there. Calling it a playroom did nothing to disguise the dank basement smell and the permanent chill. It was like playing Ping-Pong in Siberia.

The only sign of life in the kitchen was on the oversize wood table. At the head of the rectangular table, a high-backed chair was pushed away, slightly askew.

Her mother had bought the six mismatched chairs at yard sales. She'd delighted in sanding and staining each, and the contrast of each of their designs made them strangely go together in a homey kind of way.

A glass of clear soda sat on the table in front of the pushed-away chair. Kelly walked over to it. Tiny bubbles popped and floated along the surface of the fizzy lemon-lime liquid. The soda hadn't gone flat yet, Kelly realized. That meant Chrissie had just poured it. A sugar cookie lay beside the glass, a single bite taken out of it.

"Chrissie?" she called out. "You here?"

No answer.

She shrugged. Chrissie had probably gone to the bathroom or was watching TV with Ryan.

Then her eyes rested on the phone. Chrissie's cell with its distinctive holographic purple cover sat alongside the cookie. *Strange,* Kelly thought. She didn't think Chrissie ever went anywhere without her phone. Even to the bathroom.

She pulled open the refrigerator door and reviewed the contents inside. Same stuff as before. Nothing too good. She reached for the plastic bottle of soda, shut the door, and poured some into a fresh glass. She rested the bottle on the island counter.

The carbonation tickled her throat as she took the first gulp. Glass in hand, she wandered through the archway that led into the back of the family room. Ryan slumped alone on the plush overstuffed sofa, totally immersed in the action on the screen. Two greenish creatures, each with three eyes, circled a lone cow in a meadow. They prodded the animal with some sort of electric device that buzzed on contact. Then there was heated discussion about returning to the ship.

Kelly sighed. Another alien movie. Her brother had a thing for sci-fi. It was all he'd watch or read.

"Hey, spacehead," she called. "Where's Chrissie?"

Ryan grunted, barely acknowledging her presence. His eyes remained glued to the action on the screen. The cow was having convulsions.

Figures, she thought. A total TV android. Ryan was impossible to talk to with the TV on. It was as if he inhabited the weird worlds he watched.

"Fine. Be that way. See if I care." Then she heard it again.

Kelly listened as the eight-note melody repeated. It was louder than it had been upstairs, but it was the same creepy song. The tune reminded her of the music played in horror films—right before the crazy guy leaps out at the innocent girl.

It's a ringtone, she suddenly realized. And it was coming from the kitchen. She hurried back through the archway toward the noise. Then she chuckled to herself. *I'm just like the girls in those horror films,* she thought. Running toward the creepy sound. Spencer would find this funny. She couldn't wait to tell him that she had fallen into the classic scary movie trap. He was really into those old Hitchcock films.

The melody stopped as she entered the kitchen. Chrissie was back—and she was talking on her phone.

She changed her ringtone, Kelly thought. She didn't particularly like this new one. Too creepy.

Chrissie didn't notice Kelly. She stood by the kitchen table, wearing navy sweats with her feet bare. Her back was to Kelly. Listening intently to whoever was calling, she stared out the large picture window overlooking the backyard. The outdoor spotlight illuminated the swirling flakes. Large evergreens sagged under the weight of the week's snow. The yard was an expanse of white. Nobody had been out back since the last snowfall.

Chrissie whispered into her phone. Kelly couldn't make out all the words, but she sensed that her babysitter was bothered about something. Chrissie remained turned with her shoulders slumped as she whispered somberly. Eyes still focused on the empty yard, she ran her hand along the square-panel window at the top of the back door next to the window. Huge icicles hung from the archway outside the door. "No. No way," she said into the phone.

Kelly hesitated, about to speak. Then she changed her mind. Chrissie was obviously involved in a private conversation. It didn't seem right to bother her now about smelling peppermint. Down here in the warmth of the kitchen, the whole spooky-odor thing seemed silly. She drained her glass of soda, placed the empty glass quietly on the counter, and headed to her room.

"Hey, everyone," she announced into her webcam as she slid into her chair. "I'm back."

Paige lifted her head and faced her screen. "Finally! That took forever. We're totally bored. I'm even polishing my toenails."

Kelly laughed. "Wow, you really must be bored." Paige was much more the blisters-and-bandages-in-cleats type than the pedicure-ready-for-sandals girl, especially in the middle of winter.

Paige smirked. She raised one foot to the camera. "Look how I've botched it." She wiggled her toes, the blue polish thick and bumpy.

Kelly grimaced. "Maybe you need a redo?"

"Nice of you to join us." Spencer's face appeared in the bottom box on her screen. "We'd almost given up on this whole sleepover thing."

"It was your idea," Gavin pointed out. He squeezed into the frame with Spencer.

"Sorry," she said. "My bad." She watched Gavin toss pieces of popcorn in the air. Spencer bounced up to catch each kernel in his mouth.

"See, no hands!" Spencer grinned, then gulped another airborne kernel. "Party games for the sleepover."

"Excellent. Maybe we should all make popcorn," she suggested. She then looked closer at her screen. Paige was battling with the goopy polish brush and the tiny surface of her small toenails. Spencer and Gavin were performing like the seals at Sea World. But June . . . she looked closer. . . . June's frame was empty.

"June?" she called. "You there?"

June didn't respond.

"Where's June?" she asked the others.

Paige lifted her eyes from her botched pedicure. Coloring inside the lines was not her strength. "I don't know. She was there when I got back from finding the polish. I had to nab it from Chrissie's room. Don't tell her."

"June was there when we returned from the kitchen to get popcorn," Spencer added.

Kelly shrugged. June probably went to get something too.

As Spencer told a joke, though, her eyes couldn't stop wandering to the frame where June should have been. Something about it felt wrong. She just didn't know what.

Spencer was on a roll. "What did the snowman and the vampire name their baby?"

"What?" Paige abandoned the polish, leaving one set of toes in their natural state.

"Frostbite!" Spencer grinned. Everyone else groaned. He'd been telling lame jokes since they were little kids.

"I've got one," Gavin said. "What do ghosts dance to?"

"Soul music." Spencer rolled his eyes. "That one's played out."

Gavin shoved Spencer. Spencer shoved him back. Kelly ignored them. Her eyes returned to June's screen. What was it? Then it hit her. She didn't know why she hadn't noticed it right away. June's frame had gone completely red.

"What do you guys see when you look at June's frame on your screen?" she asked her friends.

Everyone stopped talking and joking.

"Weird," Paige murmured. "It's all red."

"Is her room painted red?" Gavin asked.

"No. It's yellow," Spencer answered.

"So why are we all seeing red?" Kelly asked. "I mean, shouldn't we see her vanity chair, since her computer was on her vanity? Or something in her room?"

"Maybe something's up with her computer," Spencer ventured. "A weird electrical thing?"

"Did she say where she was going?" Kelly asked.

Paige looked perplexed. "No. It was kind of like one minute she was there and then she wasn't."

"Yeah," Spencer agreed. "One time I looked up and no June. Poof!"

"June?" Kelly called again. "Are you there?"

June's window on her screen remained red and silent.

"She'll be back." Kelly relaxed and watched Spencer do an impression of their earth science teacher. His accent was a little off but still funny. Paige joined in, making them guess which teachers she was mimicking. She had the phys ed teacher's quirky tics spot-on.

"You know," Gavin said after fifteen minutes had passed, "it's weird that June still hasn't come back. Shouldn't we try to find her?"

June's screen still glowed scarlet.

"She's fine," Kelly replied, annoyed that Gavin was telling them what to do. June was their friend, not his.

Nevertheless, she reached for her cell phone and quickly texted June.

She got no response.

"I texted her," Paige announced. "She's not texting back."

"Me too. I'll call," Kelly offered. June's phone rang three times before going to voice mail. "Hey, June, it's us. Where are you? Come back to your screen or call me. Bye."

Kelly shrugged to her friends. "I left a message."

"I think Gavin's right. It's weird," Paige said.

"It is kind of spooky after the whole Miss Mary thing," Gavin put in.

Kelly laughed. "So you really fell for the bringing-back-the-dead thing?"

"Didn't you?" he asked seriously.

"No way." She recalled the peppermint scent but pushed the unsettling thought aside. A coincidence, she figured.

The abrupt slam of a door and then a violent crash thundered through the house, breaking Kelly away from her thoughts.

This wasn't something she could just block out. Kelly jumped up and raced down the stairs, unsure of what she would find.

CHAPTER 8

"What was that?" she cried, skidding from the foyer into the main entrance of the family room.

Ryan stared at the aliens on the TV, completely engrossed in the movie.

"Did you hear me?" Kelly asked her brother. "Did you hear that noise?"

Ryan didn't answer. The sofa had molded to his unmoving body the way a worn glove cradles a baseball.

"You've got to me kidding me." She groaned. "I don't know what your problem is, but I'm not playing your silent game. I can't believe you didn't hear that!" She hurried across the room and through the back entrance to the kitchen. Chrissie sat in a ladder-back chair by the table, obsessively twirling a single strand of her blond hair.

"Did you hear that noise?" Kelly demanded.

Chrissie nodded. Twirling, twirling.

Why wasn't anybody talking? Kelly wondered.

She took a closer look at her babysitter. Still in her navy sweats, Chrissie was now wearing white snow boots. Flecks of wetness dotted their nylon exterior. Her face looked pale, ashen, as if she was worried.

"What's up?" Kelly pulled out the spindle-back chair next to her and sat.

"The icicles outside the back door fell," Chrissie said without feeling. The monotone sounded strange coming from her. Kelly was used to her peppy, chirpy voice.

Kelly glanced toward the door. In the glow of the outdoor spotlight, she saw that the row of huge icicles was no longer hanging. That would account for the crashing noise, she realized. But she wondered about the slam. Someone must have slammed the door to cause the icicles to fall so suddenly. They were the thick kind. It would've taken a lot of force to smash them to the ground.

"Were you outside?" she asked Chrissie.

"No." Chrissie stared at a far-off spot on the table as if suddenly interested in the vintage woodwork.

"Really?" she pressed. The snow caked on the treads of Chrissie's boots was obvious.

"No, I wasn't." Chrissie twirled her hair, wrapping a piece tightly around her index finger. She wouldn't meet Kelly's gaze.

Chrissie was lying. Kelly could see that. But why? "Someone must have slammed the door," Kelly began.

Chrissie didn't saying anything right away. She opened her mouth as if about to, but then seemed to think better of it.

Kelly's throat felt dry. She swallowed several times. The Chrissie she knew was always bubbly and happy. She didn't recognize this morose girl sitting next to her. "Are you okay?" she asked gently.

Chrissie nodded slowly.

"Really, if you're not, you can tell me." Kelly reached out her hand to touch Chrissie's arm, but Chrissie shrank back.

"Was that your boyfriend on the phone?" *Maybe it's a breakup thing,* Kelly thought. She didn't have any experience yet with boyfriends, but she'd seen enough TV shows with girls moaning over broken hearts.

Chrissie shook her head. That wasn't it. Again she

seemed about to say something but stopped herself, casting her eyes away from Kelly.

"Seriously. You're scaring me," Kelly said in a low voice. The air around them seemed heavy. As if a dark cloud had descended on the kitchen.

"She doesn't want you downstairs," Chrissie whispered suddenly.

"What?" Kelly leaned closer.

"She won't be happy," Chrissie murmured.

Kelly swallowed hard, trying desperately to wet her throat. "Who?"

Chrissie stayed silent for a few minutes, a shadow of fear clouding her gaze. "You should go back to your room," she finally said.

What was going on? Who was Chrissie talking about? "I don't understand."

"It's best."

"*What's* best?" Kelly's voice rose unnaturally.

Chrissie twisted that one chunk of hair so taut, it was in danger of breaking. "Just go. Please."

Kelly stayed seated for a moment, contemplating her babysitter. Something was definitely wrong. She debated calling her parents. But she knew they couldn't do anything trapped in the snow except worry. That wasn't good. She gazed around the kitchen. Nothing looked different. The TV blared from the family room. The wind shook the trees outside, and the snow fell faster. Everything seemed okay—except for Chrissie.

Kelly shrugged. Sitting with Chrissie made her uncomfortable. *I'll just leave her alone,* she thought. *Let her work it out, whatever it is. Maybe Paige knows what's wrong with her crazy sister.*

"Whatever," she said, getting up. "I'll be in my room."

Chrissie stared at her blankly.

"Okay then." Kelly couldn't get back to her room fast enough. She had to talk to her friends. Tell them what was going on.

The preppy plaid of her childhood welcomed her as she entered her bedroom. For the first time in a long time, the pink and green comforted her, gave her that secure, settled feeling. Maybe she wouldn't press her mom to redecorate.

She stood in front of her desk and gazed at her screen. Her mouth opened in shock.

In the bottom frame, Gavin and Spencer appeared to be having a whispered argument. Gavin's forehead was furrowed, and his dark eyebrows were drawn together in worry. Spencer's freckles seemed to darken against his suddenly pale skin.

June's frame was red and still empty.

And Paige's frame was now empty too—and filled with the same pulsing crimson color.

"Where's Paige?" she asked hesitantly.

Gavin and Spencer whirled their heads around to face her. She could see it in their eyes. Something had happened while she was downstairs. Something bad.

"Where's Paige?" she asked again.

"She's gone," Gavin said slowly.

"Gone where?" Her voice again sounded shrill.

"Kel, something freaky is going on. We were talking to Paige, and then, boom, her screen turned bloodred and she was gone. Totally gone. As if she was sucked up by some force," Spencer babbled nervously. "We tried calling her cell. You know she always has her cell. It just kept ringing and ringing. No voice mail or anything. She won't answer texts, either."

"Maybe she just went to the bathroom or another room," Kelly suggested.

"Both of them?" Gavin asked.

She stared at her screen. Both June and Paige's frames were a hot, pulsing red. Definitely strange. A seed of dread stirred in the pit of her stomach.

She flipped open her phone and hit Paige's name in Contacts. She listened to the ringing. Eight times, she counted, before she hung up. No voice mail. She pushed June's number. Her phone rang, then clicked to voice mail. She left another message, more urgent than the one before.

Where are they? she wondered. Her fingers drummed her desk. The heater clanked overhead, working to combat the chill of the churning wind.

I NEED U TO TXT ME!!!!!! NOW!! she wrote to Paige.

She watched her screen. Paige always answered texts at lightning speed. They joked about it all the time.

Not now. No text came back.

"Kel, there's something else." Spencer leaned toward his webcam. His eyes widened in her monitor.

"Don't tell her," Gavin cautioned.

"She should know." Spencer turned to Gavin.

"I don't think so. We don't know what we're dealing with," Gavin said as if she weren't listening.

"What shouldn't I know?" she demanded.

Gavin shot Spencer a warning look, but Spencer ignored him. "While you were gone . . . right after Paige went missing . . . we heard something coming from your room."

"What do you mean?"

"Whispering. There was the sound of a voice whispering in your room," he said.

"W-what was it saying?" she stammered.

"We couldn't be sure. It sounded like . . . like . . ."

"What?" she cried.

"It sounded like 'Miss Mary, Miss Mary.'"

CHAPTER 9

A sudden chill shook Kelly's body. She shivered, pulling her hands farther into her sweatshirt sleeves. As the wind moaned through the trees, the branches slapped her window in angry protest.

This sleepover wasn't turning out as she'd planned. She wished all her friends were here with her. All together in her room, laughing with the lights on. Sitting alone in the dark in the storm was creeping her out. And she didn't get creeped out. Ever.

"Are you sure?" she asked Gavin and Spencer. She straightened in her chair, trying to shake away her nerves.

They nodded.

She eyed them suspiciously. The clanking of the

heater had stopped, and a slight chill settled over her room. She pushed the bowl of uneaten melted green ice cream to the side of her desk.

"No joke. We heard it. Really." Spencer gazed unflinchingly.

After all these years, she knew Spencer could never meet her eye if he was lying. *But just because he believes he heard something doesn't mean he really did*, she assured herself. She was afraid to let her mind go down the other path.

"I know it doesn't make sense," Gavin said. "But something is going on."

"What kind of something?" she challenged.

"Something supernatural," he said calmly.

Kelly tried to laugh, but the croak that came out sounded more as if she were choking. Her throat felt unnaturally dry again.

"I think we did it," Gavin said. "I think, somehow, we brought back the spirit of that dead girl." His eyes gleamed with excitement, although his face remained grim.

Kelly stared at both boys. Spencer looked uncomfortable. He fidgeted in his chair. He gazed around his room. But Gavin looked, well, almost energized. His wiry body fidgeted expectantly. She wasn't sure what to make of this, especially since she barely knew him.

"Do you think we did, Kelly?" Spencer asked. "Do you feel anything weird?"

She rubbed her icy fingers together, then tried to warm them with her breath. The whole night had been weird. Paige and June were missing. Chrissie was completely off-kilter. And she had felt a strange sensation after they had chanted. Electric. Dizzy. She didn't know what.

But she wasn't going to admit it.

"No." She picked up her cell and dialed Paige. Non-stop ringing. June's number went right to voice mail. She didn't bother to leave another message, although she really wanted to scream at her friend. Where was she? Why were she and Paige doing this?

"So?" Spencer asked.

"So nothing," she replied. She tried to control her frustration.

"They're not answering my texts." Spencer held his phone up to the camera as if her seeing his phone would make her realize how odd it all was.

"Mine either." She sat quietly for a minute. The air

around her had grown frigid. She could faintly see her breath as she exhaled. The upstairs heater must have died, she realized. She hoped the downstairs one was still working. It was going to be a long, uncomfortable night if they didn't have heat.

"I'm going to call Paige's house phone," she told them. She almost never called Paige at home anymore. Paige always had her cell by her side. She dialed and listened as the Coxes' phone rang and rang. Where were Paige's parents? They wouldn't be out on a night like this. On the tenth ring, she hung up.

Rummaging about on her desk, she uncovered the slim school directory under a pile of notebooks. An absurd-looking moose wearing a sports jersey graced the cover. She'd never understood why they had to have the stupidest mascot ever. She flipped to the Cs to check the number. It was silly, really. She'd known Paige since she was born. She didn't have the wrong number. She knew that. But still.

She dialed again, pressing each number deliberately. Ringing and ringing. No answer. "No one's there," she reported.

"Isn't Paige's sister babysitting you?" Gavin asked.

"Maybe she knows where Paige went."

Spencer perked up. "Yeah, Kel. You should go ask her."

Kelly sighed. "I don't know if that's the best idea right now."

"Why?" Spencer asked.

She told them about how Chrissie had lied about being outside. She explained how disturbed and disconnected she seemed.

"She's possessed," Gavin said matter-of-factly.

"Oh, please," she scoffed.

"Think about it," he challenged. "Think about when her behavior changed."

It was true. Chrissie had started acting odd after the chanting. After the smell of peppermint.

Gavin's dark-brown eyes burned through the screen at her with an intensity that made her uncomfortable. "We did something," he said.

She stood and turned her back on the boys. She needed a moment to think. To try to make sense of it all.

She walked to her bed and grabbed the wool blanket folded at the end. An Authentic Vermont Blanket, of course. She wrapped the thick, bright-green blanket around her for warmth. Moving about her room, she came up with plenty of places her friends could have gone. She just couldn't come up with a lot of reasons why they hadn't returned her texts or answered their phones.

Pulling back her shade, she gazed at the falling snow. Frost inched up the windowpane. It was going to be a big storm, she realized. Her mother had been right. She hoped her parents were okay. She hadn't heard from them in a couple of hours.

She crossed her room and flicked on her light. The glow brightened the room and her mood. Her friends' disappearances suddenly seemed less scary. *There is an explanation,* she told herself. *I just have to figure it out.*

She glanced back at her monitor. Only Spencer's face was visible in the frame. Gavin didn't seem to be around. Spencer waved his hand, beckoning to her urgently.

She hurried back to her desk.

"I need to talk to you," he whispered. His eyes darted about anxiously. "Turn off your microphone. Use the keyboard."

She gave him a questioning look but followed his instructions.

Kookykell2011: WHAT'S WRONG?

SpenceX77: IT'S GAVIN.

Kookykell2011: ??? WHERE IS HE?

SpenceX77: WENT TO GET A DRINK. DON'T HAVE MUCH TIME. I'M REALLY FREAKED OUT.

Kookykell2011: ABOUT MISS MARY?

SpenceX77: WELL, YEAH, BUT ABOUT GAVIN, TOO.

Kookykell2011: WHY?

SpenceX77: IDK. IT'S A VIBE. HE'S ACTING REALLY STRANGE.

Kookykell2011: STRANGE HOW?

SpenceX77: NERVOUS. TWITCHY.

Kookykell2011: MAYBE THAT'S WHAT HE'S LIKE.

SpenceX77: THAT'S NOT IT. STARTED WITH THE MISS MARY THING. BEEN WEIRD SINCE. KEEPS MUMBLING STUFF UNDER HIS BREATH. TO HIMSELF, BUT I CAN HEAR. IT'S SCARING ME.

Kookykell2011: WHAT'S HE SAYING?

SpenceX77: STUFF THAT DOESN'T MAKE SENSE. COLDNESS IS COMING AND YOU CAN'T BE HERE.

Kookykell2011: WHO CAN'T?

SpenceX77: IDK. HE DOESN'T SEEM IN CONTROL. IT'S AS IF HE CAN'T HELP SAYING THIS STUFF OR HE DOESN'T KNOW HE'S MUTTERING IT OR—

Kookykell2011: WAIT. IT'S LIKE—

Kelly stopped typing. She tried to swallow but couldn't. Her lungs felt as if they were being squeezed. She recalled the strange things that Chrissie had muttered just a few minutes ago. She hadn't told Gavin and Spencer what Chrissie had said. So why was Gavin saying the same sort of things?

She sucked in air, trying to inflate her lungs. To breathe normally again. In and out.

Kookykell2011: R u sure?
SpenceX77: Yes!!!
Kookykell2011: Maybe he's playing you. . . .

She kept coming back to her know-all-the-facts nature. She didn't buy into fortune-tellers and horoscopes and the other mystical things some of her friends believed. She liked science and reasoning. Everything for her always had a factual explanation. That was why she liked scaring her friends so much. All that supernatural stuff was fake, and she knew it.

Tonight was the first time she was having trouble making sense of things.

SpenceX77: Maybe. I barely know the guy. I don't want him here anymore. Something about him is way off. I don't trust him.

Kookykell2011: I agree. Been feeling that way all night.

SpenceX77: What do I do?

She wasn't sure. Maybe Spencer could fake sickness and ask Gavin to go home. She wished June would show herself. She was the best at these kinds of schemes. She'd create a believable story of why Gavin had to leave.

Kelly glanced at Spencer's webcam frame to judge how worried he was. She froze.

A dark shadow loomed behind her friend.

Spencer had no idea. His eyes stayed focused on his keyboard. He was typing. She stared in horror as the figure glided closer. She wanted to scream but could only watch in mute terror as it reached out its arms and slowly brought them down . . . down . . . toward Spencer's neck.

She had to warn him. She had barely seconds before . . . Her fingers flew across the keyboard.

She was too late. The attacker wrapped both hands around Spencer's bare neck. His fingers squeezed . . . squeezed . . . squeezed the air from Spencer's throat.

"Noooo! Stop!" she cried. Then she remembered their microphones were off. Spencer couldn't hear her. She grabbed her computer with both hands and shook it hard, as if she could somehow stop the horror with the force of her fear. She couldn't just sit here and watch her friend suffocate!

She wanted to cover her face, but she was afraid to let poor Spencer out of her sight. She stared in total helplessness as he weakened, growing limp.

Suddenly Spencer's eyes bulged. He twisted his body with a burst of renewed strength, jerking it left and right. The attacker's grip loosened, and he leaned toward Spencer.

Kelly narrowed her eyes and gripped her desk to steady herself. She stared at the face of Spencer's attacker. It was a face she recognized.

CHAPTER 10

Spencer jumped up and pushed his attacker back. Then he spun to face him.

Gavin.

Gavin's sinewy face broke into a huge grin. He laughed. "Oh, man. I totally scared you. Score!" He pumped his fist in victory.

"That was so not funny!" Spencer spat.

"It was just a joke."

Spencer's cheeks reddened slightly, but he forced a strained smile. "Y-yeah, you got me."

Gavin ran his hand through his spiky hair. "Who did you think it was, dude?"

Spencer shrugged. Kelly could sense him shrinking back as if he was putting up an invisible wall. It felt peculiar to sit across the street and watch the scene play out. Almost like watching a scary movie and not being able to help the victim.

"You are such a wimp," Gavin said. He gave Spencer a shove. Then another.

Kelly winced. She knew guys shoved all the time. Yet with Gavin, she wondered if there wasn't more to it. True, Spencer was way bigger than Gavin, but he was the kind of mellow kid who set ants free instead of squishing them. Gavin, though, had a barely contained aggression that pulsed right below the surface of his skin. She watched, still helpless, as Spencer backed himself up to the desk. She wasn't sure what he was doing. Was Gavin advancing on him?

For a moment, her screen was filled only by the heathered gray fabric of Spencer's T-shirt.

"Spencer!" she screamed. Was Gavin hurting him? Had he pushed him against the desk and hit him?

Then she heard a blip. SPENCEX77 IS OFFLINE appeared on her chat screen. His face slid into view, unharmed. She sighed, realizing that he'd blocked his screen so he could exit out of their conversation before Gavin saw it. She exited too and turned her microphone on. She was glad he hadn't heard her scream.

"Kelly? You there?" Spencer asked from the bottom frame. Gavin stood alongside him. The frames on her screen where June and Paige should have been continued to pulse red. *Danger.* The word suddenly popped into her head. Red is the color of danger.

"Yeah, I'm—" Her screen suddenly went blank.

Wrapping the wool blanket tighter around her, she pressed enter. The webcam sleepover didn't come back.

Her computer was still on. So were her lights. They hadn't lost power, she realized. She gazed at the screen. CONNECTION IS TEMPORARILY UNAVAILABLE. Her Internet service was down.

The wind slammed against the house, rattling the trees. The frozen branches clawed angrily at the siding. She fiddled with her modem, hoping she could bring up the connection. The storm might have shut it down for the night.

She watched the Internet icon at the bottom of the screen. It blinked, trying to connect.

Internet down, she texted to Spencer. U OK?

MINE DOWN 2, he replied quickly. But he didn't answer her question.

She waited, watching the blinking icon search for a

signal, desperately wondering what was going on across the street. The scene kept replaying in her mind. She knew what she'd seen. It hadn't been a joke——no matter what Gavin said or how much he laughed. Gavin really seemed as if he was going to strangle Spencer. The glare in his eyes wasn't the look of someone joking. It was danger- ous. Unhinged. If Spencer hadn't fought back and turned around when he did . . . She shuddered to think about it.

After what felt like an eternity, although it was really only a few minutes, the Internet icon flashed green. She was back online. She signed in to the webcam confer- ence. Biting her lip, she wondered what she would find. Would Spencer be okay? Would June and Paige be back?

A single frame popped onto her screen.

The camera focused in on Spencer and Gavin sit- ting side by side. Spencer's posture seemed much more relaxed. Gavin leaned back casually in his chair. Every- thing appeared okay between them. They seemed like buddies again.

Her eyes roamed her screen. The frames where June and Paige had been——the frames that had turned bright red——were no longer there. She tried to dial into their computers. The connection failed repeatedly. No one was at the other end to link into the videoconference site.

"Can you guys see June and Paige's frames?" she asked. The panic began brewing again in her stomach. The red frames were disturbing, but at least they had been something. A lifeline of some sort. Without them, she felt very far away from her friends.

Spencer shook his head. "They disappeared. Can you see them?"

"Nope." She glanced at her cell phone. No texts. No messages. "I think we need to do something."

"There's nothing to do," Gavin replied.

"That's so wrong!" she cried. She'd had enough of him. Her fear and frustration bubbled up, congealing into anger toward him. "You barely even know us! And you have no idea where my friends are. I'm going to find them, and you can't stop me!"

Gavin threw up his arms in mock surrender.

"Calm down, Kel," Spencer said. "You're right. We need to do something. But this webcam thing isn't working."

"What do you mean?"

"Something is wrong. We need to figure this out together. Gavin and I will come over there. We'll all sit down—Chrissie, too—and make a plan."

"Good idea," she agreed. She wasn't thrilled about Gavin coming too, but decided not let that get to her. She wanted company. "Hurry, okay?"

Spencer nodded. "Be over in a sec." He logged off.

She left her chair and flopped onto her bed. The chill had completely invaded her room, making her long to snuggle under her plaid comforter. She resisted. Spencer and Gavin would be here in a moment. She waited.

And waited.

She rolled over, watching the clock on her bedside table. Ten minutes had passed since Spencer had logged off. She wondered what was taking so long. She pulled her sleeping bag off the floor and draped it over herself. Staring at her ceiling, she let five more minutes pass. Then she sat upright.

Spencer had been running across the street to her house since they were in kindergarten. It took two minutes, at most.

She flipped open her phone. WHERE R U??? she texted.

She waited. No reply. No ringing doorbell. Nothing.

Maybe he's waiting at the door, she thought. *Maybe the doorbell is busted.* She leaped off her bed. How horrible of her to leave them outside in the brewing storm. She raced out of her room and down the hall. At the top of the stairs, she stopped.

The smell.

The bracing scent hung thickly in the air. She stood startled, as if slapped in the face. Every nerve tingled as she inhaled.

Peppermint. Again.

No one was in the hallway. The stairs were empty. She couldn't explain where the mysterious odor was coming from. Suddenly, more than ever, it felt urgent that Spencer be at the door. She needed him to smell the smell. To tell her she wasn't going crazy. To explain everything.

She hurried down the steps.

The temperature change was obvious as she reached the foyer. The heat was still on down here. The murmur of the TV reached her ears from the family room. She could still smell the peppermint, although perhaps more faintly than before.

Twisting the lock on the front door, she reached for the brass handle. She pulled hard. An enormous gust of frigid air swept through the house as she opened the door onto the storm. Her hair flew about her face, and she leaned into the wind.

The front step was empty.

No Spencer or Gavin.

The outside lights on either side of the door cast a faint glow on the inky darkness of the night. Snow swirled about—the fat flakes carried in circles by the incredible wind.

She peered down the deserted walkway. It was covered by an untouched layer of fresh whiteness. No boot prints. They hadn't tried to come up to the door.

Still inside the house, she tried to see across the desolate street. The neighborhood was quiet, except for the howls of the wind. Everyone was inside, protected from the oncoming storm. She stared at the outline of Spencer's house. A shiver ran along the base of her neck.

The house was dark. Completely dark.

Twisting her head, she tried for a different angle. Her eyes teared from the icy gusts. But no matter how hard she squinted, the Stones' house continued to blend in with the blackness of the sky. No lights were on. No lights inside. No lights outside.

It was as if no one was home.

As if no one had ever been there.

The house was totally abandoned.

CHAPTER 11

Kelly slowly shut the front door. She stood motionless on the woven mat, trying to piece together the puzzle.

Spencer and Gavin had been in their house a few minutes ago. She was sure of it. And Spencer's little brother Charlie had been home too. And Spencer's mom. They wouldn't all leave suddenly in the night, would they?

As hard as she tried, she couldn't come up with a reasonable explanation. At this point, she was even willing to take sort-of reasonable. Maybe they all decided to go to sleep and shut every light—even the outside ones? Doubtful. Especially since Spencer had promised to run right over.

She hooked her mind around the promise. Of all her friends, Spencer was the one she could count on most to keep a promise. If he said he was coming, then he'd be here. He always came through. She would wait.

The hum of the television penetrated her muddled thoughts.

Ryan. She'd go hang out with Ryan until Spencer showed up, she decided.

She entered the family room from the foyer. The overhead light blazed brightly in here, and the heat seeped through the vents. Her mother had a passion for Americana crafts. A painting of an American flag done on a large, weathered, wooden plank hung over the sofa. The other walls held needlepoint reproductions of colonial samplers. Carved, narrow benches and corn-husk dolls decorated the area near the stone fireplace. On most other nights, Kelly felt as if she were living in a museum. She often teased her mom about it, calling it "Ye Olde Family Room." But tonight being surrounded by all her mother's trinkets felt soothing.

Ryan sat on the sofa, exactly in the same position as before.

"Hey," she said.

He continued to stare at the TV.

She was about to make a sarcastic remark about

whatever alien sci-fi movie he was captivated by when she stopped—and took a second look at the screen.

Three women in shorts and colorful tank tops stood in a row. They squatted in unison. Together they kicked their legs and counted the repetitions. Was Ryan really watching an exercise show?

She examined the women for another minute. They weren't even young or cool-looking. They looked like her grandmother's friends.

"Hey, you, why are you watching this?" she asked.

Ryan didn't answer. His eyes never left the screen. He appeared mesmerized by the middle-aged women, who were now jogging in place. Retro eighties music played in the background, but the women were hopelessly off the beat. There was absolutely nothing interesting in this show. And it wasn't bad enough to be funny. It was just bad.

Kelly narrowed her gaze at her brother. She was so not in the mood for his tricks. "Answer me," she demanded.

He stayed mute. Unmoving.

She studied him. Was this a joke?

"Stop it, Ryan." She waved her hands in front of his

unblinking brown eyes. He didn't flinch.

"Can you hear me?" she cried. Her heart began to beat rapidly. From anger. From confusion. "Move!" she screamed, her face centimeters from his. "Move!"

He remained frozen. She could hear him breathing. The air slowly traveling in and out of his nostrils. She grabbed his shoulders with both her hands and shook him hard. Again and again. "Answer me!" she screamed frantically.

His body felt limp in her hands. He gave no resistance. His glassy eyes focused vacantly on the TV. The three women crossed their arms and legs, counting out the fifteenth jumping jack. Their perky voices filled the silence of the room.

Her heart beat all over her body. Her thoughts jumbled around her brain. Nothing was making sense. Why was Ryan like this? It was almost as if he was . . . as if he was . . .

She hesitated, not wanting to complete the horrible thought. Fearful that if she thought it, it would be true. For the only thing she could come up with was that Ryan was . . . possessed.

She stared suspiciously at his zombielike figure.

He had never acted like this before. "Ryan." Her voice came out as a whisper. "Ryan, please." She could no longer disguise her fear. "You're freaking me out. Please."

He didn't respond to her pleas. Immobile, he stared into nothingness. Vacant.

She needed help. Now. She knew that.

She pulled her phone out of her pocket. Her fingers automatically dialed her mom's cell.

"Hi, sweetie." Her mom's voice, so near yet so far, made her legs weak.

"Hi, Mom." Her voice caught, and she swallowed hard.

"Is everything okay? What are you doing?" The line crackled.

"Well, you see—" Static filled the airwaves, then disappeared. It disguised the terror in her voice.

Kelly hesitated. She started to tell her mother that everything wasn't okay. That their babysitter was depressed. That her friends weren't texting her. That the house smelled weird. That her brother had become a zombie.

No. She couldn't tell her all that. She was the one who would sound crazy. Besides, what did she expect

93

her mother to do so far away? She'd totally freak out and insist on driving home in this weather.

"Fine," she answered instead. "Everything's fine. Just watching TV."

"Good. Stay inside. The weather's bad." Her mom went on to tell her about the motel room and the lack of little shampoo bottles, soap, and shower caps in the bathroom. She hated motels without amenities. "Does Chrissie want to talk to me?"

Her mother's voice faded in and out. The line buzzed with static.

That was it! Chrissie would help, Kelly realized. She might be acting a little strange but she was older. She'd know what to do. She would confide in Chrissie. She didn't have to worry her mother.

"Can you hear me? Kelly, are you there?"

"We have a bad connection," she said. "I'll call back later. Everything's okay. Love you." She clicked the phone off, even though she suspected the call was dropped before she'd said good-bye.

With a backward glance at her brother—still sitting, still staring—she tucked her phone back into her pocket and headed across the room to the archway that connected the family room with the kitchen. Even from here, she could see the kitchen was dark. Was Chrissie even in there?

The babysitter's name formed on her lips, but she didn't call it out. She suddenly had the strangest sensation that she shouldn't scream. Slowly she treaded silently toward the entrance.

A breeze wafted across her body. She shivered. Where was the cold air coming from? What was in the kitchen?

She tiptoed into the darkened room. A biting coldness descended on her. Goose bumps tingled her skin. All the lights were off. But even in the dimness, she sensed that something wasn't right. The wind that had been beating against her bedroom window reached out its powerful arms and grabbed at her. The force of an unexplained squall pulled her farther into the kitchen.

She reached instinctively for the switch on the wall. Instantly the kitchen was bathed in the artificial overhead light.

Kelly clapped her hand over her mouth in complete amazement.

Her eyes followed the paper tornado churning about

the room, as if guided by a supernatural hand. White napkins rose to the ceiling, then circled back around, dipping down before another gust lifted them again. Sheets of paper—lined notebook paper, colorful school flyers, old receipts—twirled across the floor and the table. The lighter pieces joined the napkins in a crazy Tilt-A-Whirl of motion.

Kelly's gaze darted to her mother's desk. The surface was wiped clear by the windstorm vacuum. The piles of paper were now airborne.

The back door banged savagely against the wall. The door itself lay wide open to the approaching storm and the night. The wind rushed into the house as if shooting through a tunnel.

After a few seconds of shock, Kelly jumped into action. Racing across the kitchen, brushing the paper out of her path, she pushed at the door. The wind created a force she had to blindly throw her full weight against. As the door latch finally clicked into place, the paper storm died. Napkins fluttered lazily to the floor.

Kelly lay, panting, with her back against the door and surveyed the mess before her. Paper littered the kitchen. A cold wetness seeped through her fuzzy socks, chilling her toes. She gazed down. Small puddles of water dotted the floor near the door. Why had the door been wide open?

"Chrissie?" The urge to scream that she had suppressed only a few minutes ago let loose. "Chrissie! Chrissie!"

Her cries echoed through the empty house.

"Chrissie! Where are you?"

Only the faint undertones of Madonna's singing and the women counting off lunges on the TV could be heard.

The cool glass of the door's small window sent a shock through her body. Every nerve was alert.

What now? she wondered. *What do I do now?*

Her frantic gaze circled back to her mother's desk. With a jolt, she realized that the desk wasn't completely cleared of all its papers. She blinked in disbelief as she noticed one piece of paper sitting directly in the center, as if carefully placed or somehow attached.

She made her way through the carpet of trash and stood before the desk. Its distressed painted wood gleamed in the light. She rested both palms on the surface. Bending down, she stared at the lone paper.

The chills ricocheted throughout her body in an electric current much like the one she'd felt earlier in the night.

She carefully placed one finger on the paper. It yielded to her slight push. It wasn't taped into place. It stood squarely on the desk as if held there by unseen hands.

She wanted to flee but couldn't move. An energy—a force—pulled her toward the paper.

Down, down.

Kelly stared at the face on the page. The soulful eyes beckoned to her once again. The rest of the world faded into the distance. She and the girl were together. One. A bond unbreakable.

"Hello, Mary," she whispered.

CHAPTER 12

Mary Owens. The newspaper clipping that had once hung on her mother's bulletin board—the one she vividly remembered pinning up there just that afternoon—rested on the empty desk.

She couldn't explain how it had gotten there or how it had stayed there, but suddenly she felt sure of one thing: She and her friends had called back Mary's spirit. Upstairs, together, they had summoned the unhappy soul of a girl who had died a horrible, suffocating death.

Miss Mary, Miss Mary. She remembered how they'd chanted, their voices growing louder and louder.

And now all her friends were missing.

And her babysitter.

And her brother . . . was no more than a hollow shell.

Her hand rested on the receiver of the house phone. She would call the police. They would help her. They would *have* to.

Lifting the receiver to her ear, she listened to the steady buzz of the dial tone.

Did the supernatural count as an emergency? She feared they would laugh at her almost as much as she feared staying by herself in this house. She pictured the police cars skidding up the driveway. The blaring sirens and flashing lights rousing the neighbors. People gathering on the lawn, watching in curious fascination as the officers stormed the house. And she would tell them all about what had been going on tonight.

Bad idea, she knew.

Kelly gently returned the receiver to the base.

She wiggled her toes against the dampness of her socks and thought about the puddles by the door. *Maybe Chrissie went out,* she thought. She'd been wearing boots— and she certainly had been outside earlier. Chrissie could have left the door open by mistake. That was it.

An encouraging warmth spread throughout her body as the explanation unfurled in her brain. It was the same feeling she'd gotten when, at age five, her father reached for her mittened hand with an everything-will-be-okay smile every time she fell learning how to ski. She was overreacting, that was all.

She flung open the back door. The force of the wind struck her full on. Strands of hair blew about her face. She pushed them away from her eyes. Turning on all the lights in the yard, she saw that the snow hadn't begun falling too thickly yet.

She scanned the yard. The snow by the door looked trampled and kicked about. There was no question now that someone had been outside. A set of boot prints led away from the house, zigzagging across the white expanse. The tracks disappeared into the darkness. The spotlights attached to the back of the house shone only a short distance. There was no telling where the tracks led.

Still safely planted inside the doorway, Kelly scrutinized the boot prints. They weren't the deliberate prints of someone walking slowly through the snow. They were smeared and very close together. The snow was more compacted at the front of the boot print. The person had barely pressed any weight on the heel. Excess snow sprayed around the back of each print. She understood immediately. The person had been running. Fast.

Was it Chrissie? It had to be, she reasoned.

But why was she running? Was she running to something? Or was she being chased?

"Chrissie? Chrissie? Are you out there?" she yelled into the darkness.

The wind swallowed her cries.

"Chrissie?"

Her voice echoed back to her. Her throat grew dry and scratchy again. Panic pushed its way up.

The snowflakes fell silently from the sky. The yard remained frozen and eerily quiet.

Why would Chrissie leave?

"Ryan!" she screamed. "Ryan, can you hear me? This is an emergency!"

She waited. The television hummed in the house behind her. Her brother didn't come.

She strained her ears, hoping against hope that Spencer and Gavin would ring the doorbell. Everything would be okay if they'd just show up, she decided. As hard as she tried, she couldn't will the doorbell to ring.

She was overcome by the need to do something. She was fed up with waiting. Waiting for her friends to show up. Waiting to understand what was going on.

Her father's black rubber snow boots sat to the right of the door. He'd been outside shoveling yesterday. Suddenly it seemed like years since she'd seen her parents.

She peeled off her damp socks and shoved her feet into the oversize boots. The nubby, frayed lining scratched her toes. The boots were far too big, but she didn't want to waste time running to the front hall to look for her own boots. She grabbed her green parka with the faux-fur-trimmed hood off the back of the chair she'd thrown it on earlier. She pulled it on, not bothering to trouble with the zipper. She stepped outside, closing the door tightly behind her.

For a moment she stood, trying to formulate a plan.

But she realized she had none. The plan was to find Chrissie. Beyond that, she had no idea.

Unaccustomed to the weight of her father's boots, she wobbled as she moved into the snow. The frozen top layer crunched as her soles broke through it. The wet, heavy snow and the weight of the wind made each step forward feel as if she were pushing against a brick wall.

The cold cut through her thin flannel pajama pants, stinging her legs. She shoved her bare fingers deep into her parka pockets. Swirling snowflakes coated her hair.

Huddling against the cold, she pushed on.

Stepping in the boot prints left by Chrissie made walking easier. She placed each foot carefully, working her way farther and farther from the warmth and safety of the house.

The shadows of the trees tilted over the snow-covered yard, making it hard to follow the prints. She squinted through the frozen flakes lining her lashes. The light from the house grew dimmer and dimmer as she trudged forward. The moonless sky cast no light on her path.

Kelly concentrated on following the prints. Up, over, and down, she dragged each heavy boot. Her hot breath came out in puffs against the cold night air. Her cheeks tingled painfully. She knew they must be bright red.

"Chrissie?" she called again and again.

The wind howled mournfully. The trees shook their snow-caked branches at her. Never before had she felt more alone.

She shivered and dug her hands deeper into her pockets. She leaned into the gusting wind. Print after print. She followed the path, each step bring her closer to . . .

"Chrissie!"

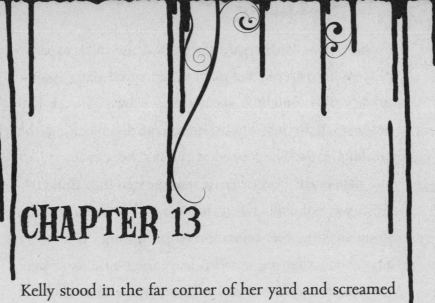

CHAPTER 13

Kelly stood in the far corner of her yard and screamed her babysitter's name. "Where are you?"

She stared blindly at the snow.

There were no more prints.

Gone. The prints were gone.

The vast whiteness stretched unbroken by human feet. Turning in a slow circle, she squinted through the steady snowflakes. Though there was only the slightest glimmer of light this far from the house, she was sure: The boot prints had abruptly stopped.

Forbidding darkness pushed toward her from the evergreen-lined edges of her large yard. She wished she had thought to bring a flashlight. The pines whispered, warning her away.

She knew Paige's yard lay behind the thick expanse of trees her parents had planted years and years ago for privacy. But tonight it seemed miles away. She shaded her eyes with her hands, momentarily blocking the blinding snow. She looked at the last boot print. What had happened? Had Chrissie disappeared into thin air?

A wave of chills raced through Kelly's body, and she stood shaking. She remembered promising her mother after school that she wouldn't leave the house. Now here she was in the darkness, in the snow, outside, alone. If she had known back then how the night would turn out, she would've made her parents take a dogsled back home.

Turning, she began to trudge back the way she'd come. She kept her head down, eyes on the snow. She focused only on the warmth and light of her house. Everything else was too horrible. It was better not to think about it. Just move forward.

She had gone only a few feet when she heard the noise. A movement. A faint rustling in the trees. She jerked up her head, suddenly alert. The rushing wind made it hard to hear. She waited as the wind enfolded her, whistling about her. The gale skidded the fresh snow about the yard like a desert sandstorm. A covering of white dusted over her big black boots. She bowed her head, protecting herself from the icy squall.

Everything was silent again.

She began to move forward. One step, then two. And then the unmistakable crunch of snow, coming from her right.

She was not alone.

Kelly sucked in her breath, not daring to move a muscle. She stayed rooted to her spot in the snow.

Crunch. Crunch.

The movement was deliberate. Was it an animal? she wondered. She gritted her teeth, staring into the never-ending blackness. What kind of animal? *Please let it be something small,* she thought.

She squinted into the darkness, but she couldn't make out anything. The shadows morphed about her. Varying tones of gray and black obscured all objects in the yard. The branches bent and swayed under the weight of the wind. She focused through the falling snow on the tree line to her right. A thick row of pines bordered her family's property with their neighbor's. Something was working its way through the pines. Steadily crunching. Its steps heavy. It wasn't a small animal, that was for sure.

She eyed the distance to her house. The yellow glow of the light shining through the large kitchen window suddenly seemed miles away. She knew, though, that it was only about sixty yards. Safety wasn't far.

The movement in the trees grew louder. Heading her way. For a moment, she wondered if it was Chrissie.

"Chrissie? Is that you?" Her voice sounded thin in the wind. "Are you out there?"

She shivered and listened. The movement quickened. Thudding steps of some kind. Too heavy for slight Chrissie. Whatever it was, it was big—and heading for her. "No!" she cried. The force of her scream took her by surprise, waking her from an almost trancelike state.

Her feet started before her brain could catch up. She ran through the snow. She had to get away. Her father's big, heavy boots felt like cement slippers, weighing her down. Each step required extreme effort. Pulling the boot up, out, and over, then sinking back into the wet snow. Her legs trembled. Sweat trickled between her shoulder blades and coated her skin, leaving her clammy.

She pushed forward, running. The footsteps in the trees quickened their pace, and all at once she knew. She was being chased.

With a crash of branches, the something broke free of the trees and thundered across the open yard. Within seconds, it was behind her.

Kelly panted, struggling to breathe. All her energy was directed toward moving her feet. Faster. Faster. She had to get away—had to get back to her house. Her left boot stuck in the snow. She wobbled, and her knees began to buckle. She threw her arms forward to break her fall.

No, no, no, no! her brain screamed. If she fell, it would be all over.

She managed to right herself and regain her balance. The footsteps crunched faster through the snow behind her. Closer now. She could hear the creature's breath exploding in jagged puffs. So near. She wanted to look back but knew she couldn't risk it. She had to keep going.

Her chest heaved as she ran. Her side knotted in pain, but she could see the door now. The window with its glow of safety. Only feet away.

And then she was there.

Her hand reached for the door handle, and she twisted anxiously. Her frigid fingers, white with cold, slid about on the cold metal. At first nothing happened. Dread overcame her, as she tried the handle again. Twisting and twisting. It wouldn't budge.

She frantically twisted the other way. It was stuck.

She was locked out.

She felt the creature's hot breath on her neck. She gulped, alarm overtaking her body. She squeezed the handle, refusing to let go of her way in.

"Please, oh, please," she whispered.

"Kelly, it's me."

She spun around. "Gavin! You almost gave me a heart attack."

"Sorry." His cheeks shone bright pink from the cold, but he wore a black parka and gloves. "Why were you running?"

Kelly hesitated, uncertain how to explain. "I was looking for Chrissie. She's gone. She disappeared in the snow out there."

Gavin nodded. He didn't seem surprised. He waited, not speaking.

She gazed over his shoulder, back toward the pine trees. "Where's Spencer?" Her hopes lifted at the thought of seeing her friend. She knew he'd keep his promise.

"I don't know," he said flatly.

"What do you mean?"

He shrugged. "I mean I don't know." His gaze jumped to her hand still gripping the door handle. "I'm freezing. Can we go inside?"

As much as she wanted to get inside, out of the wind and snow, she suddenly wasn't sure that she wanted Gavin inside with her. She squinted at him. "What's going on, Gavin? Where's Spencer?"

Just then a muffled noise broke through the whistling wind. She strained to hear. A song . . . no, it was a melody repeating.

The haunting melody from Chrissie's phone.

She listened closer to be sure. The muted, evil melody had to be coming from inside.

"Do you hear that?" she asked.

"Yeah." He took a step closer. "You should open the door."

"I think I locked myself out." She stayed where she was, blocking the path between him and the door.

She thought of Mary. Trapped in the snow. Freezing to death slowly, painfully. The snow draining the warmth out of her. Was that what was going to happen to her, too? Locked out in the snow . . . But how did Gavin fit in? Was he here to save her? Or was he here to—

She could no longer hear the melody. The phone had stopped ringing.

"Kelly, let's go inside," Gavin said. He stomped his boots impatiently in the snow. "Move over. Let me try."

She couldn't stay outside in this horrible cold. She knew that. "Where's Spencer?" she demanded again, refusing to move.

"He was behind me when we crossed the street. And then I looked back and he wasn't there," Gavin explained.

"But that was a long time ago," she said suspiciously. "You guys left his house a long time ago."

"I know."

"What were you doing sneaking around my yard in the dark?" She couldn't figure out what Gavin was doing here. Alone. Without Spencer.

"I wasn't sneaking around. I was searching for him."

"But you were chasing *me*."

"Because you started running." He stepped forward, and she let him pass. She wasn't sure what to do. Indecisive, she stood meekly behind him and watched over his shoulder.

He tried the handle. The cold metal slipped through his nylon gloves. He pulled off his gloves and shoved them into his parka pocket. Then he blew on his hands and rubbed them together. His hot breath loosened his fingers.

He tried the handle again. He threw what little weight he had into the door and twisted.

The door swung open.

They both nearly fell inside, stumbling into the brightness. Kelly closed the door behind them, shutting out the storm.

The house was quiet.

She blinked hard at the empty room. Her stomach dropped with disappointment. She'd secretly hoped that everything would have returned to normal—that she would have opened the door and been greeted by Chrissie and Ryan. That life would've gone back to the way it had been before she'd decided to play that silly game with her friends.

She shrugged off her coat and the boots, now dripping with snow. Her flannel pants clung damply to her legs. The front of her shirt was wet from where she had failed to zip her jacket. The chill of the storm clung to her. She longed to take a hot bath and wrap herself in her warm, fuzzy robe.

She scanned the kitchen, still littered with the contents of her mother's desk, for Chrissie's phone. She didn't see it anywhere.

The sound of someone behind her jerked her away from her thoughts. For a moment, she'd forgotten about Gavin.

He still wore his damp black parka, although his boots now lay beside hers. His white athletic socks were frayed at the heels. He stood, hands buried in his pockets, and watched her.

She stared at him for a few minutes, trying to figure out if she trusted him. His eyes held that same intensity that had unnerved her earlier in the night. He blinked several times in uncontrolled spasms. He seemed to give off an electric-like current that made the little hairs on her arms stand on edge.

Using her fingers, she brushed through her damp, tangled hair, slicking it back from her face. "So you don't know where Spencer is?" she asked again.

"No."

"June or Paige?"

"No." He gazed at her with glassy eyes. "It's just you and me now."

CHAPTER 14

"Coldness is coming," Gavin continued, his voice drained of all emotion.

"Huh? What are you talking about?" She gulped, trying to control the trembling in her voice as she remembered what Spencer had told her earlier about Gavin acting strangely.

"It's so cold out there. In the snow. Cold and dark." His voice was flat. His brown eyes held a haunted, far-away look.

"Y-yeah. Yeah, it is." Kelly stared in horror at him.

"You can't be here," he told her.

"What? Why not?" she demanded brusquely, but the squeaking of her voice betrayed her panic.

"So what should we do?" he asked suddenly. His tone

had changed abruptly, as if life had been injected back into it.

"About what?" She looked around. If she needed to, her best bet would be to run for the front door, she decided. She had a good twenty pounds on Gavin. *I could push him down,* she thought. *He may be crazy, but he doesn't look too strong.*

"I don't really know where to look for him anymore. I've been all over. I even went back to Spencer's house. It's like . . ." He hesitated, and his shoulders slumped. "It's like Spencer, his mom, his brother . . . It's like they completely disappeared."

"It's weird," she agreed. She took several steps backward, away from him. Flipping open her phone, she checked desperately for messages. Nothing. Not even a text. "Maybe they'll answer now," she said hopefully, more to herself than to him. She kept her eyes trained on Gavin as she tried each of her friends' phones again. She listened to them ring. Two rings. Five. Eight. No one was answering.

She and Gavin really were all alone.

That was when she noticed the silence.

The TV was quiet.

Had Ryan turned it off? Maybe he had snapped out of his trance.

"Ryan?" she called. She hurried toward the family room, leaving Gavin behind. Her bare feet slapped against the wooden floor. She burst inside.

And stared.

The room was empty. The television was dark. She could make out the faint impression of Ryan's legs on the overstuffed sofa cushions, but he wasn't there. No one was.

"Ryan!" she called again. She felt as if she'd been calling for people all night.

Silence once more.

Her heart began to beat so fast she was sure it might burst. The room started to spin. Slowly at first, but soon the colonial crafts were in full whirl. The floor tilted toward the ceiling. She had to sit.

She dropped into a blue gingham armchair near the sofa. The checkered pattern danced before her. She tried not to let the panic overwhelm her.

She had to find her brother.

She was in charge of him even though her parents had hired Chrissie. Not that she had done any good tonight.

She wondered what happened to a person's body once he or she was snatched by a spirit. Did the spirit claim just the person's soul or their whole being, too? And why had Mary—assuming it *was* Mary—come for everyone except her? Was she next?

And then she thought of Gavin. He was here too.

She remembered the bizarre things Gavin had been muttering. *Coldness is coming* and all that. What did it mean? Could the spirit of dead Mary have somehow gone into Gavin's body? And through him preyed, one by one, on her friends . . . ?

She shook her head violently. She had to stop thinking such crazy thoughts. Gavin was just a boy. A friend of Spencer's. Maybe he was little weird, but that was all. She had to get a grip.

A small moan escaped her throat. She had so many questions. She tried to order her thoughts. She gazed about the room, the dizziness going away.

She sensed him before she saw him. Gavin stood in the doorway, silently watching her. He waited and said nothing. She could feel the force of his gaze penetrating the back of her head. She willed herself not to acknowledge him, not to turn toward him. She didn't like him.

She wasn't going to obsess about why. He was probably harmless, but she couldn't handle his weirdness right now.

She stood shakily, holding the upholstered arm of the chair for support. She rested her phone on the cushioned seat. Then she walked to the television and stood directly before it. She raised her palm to the screen. It still felt warm. Ryan had been here not too long ago.

Upstairs. That was it. She sighed with relief. Ryan had probably gone upstairs to bed. She wanted to slap herself for being so silly.

"You okay?"

She turned toward him. Gavin had taken off his parka and was wearing the same T-shirt and jeans from earlier.

"I need to find my brother," she murmured, not meeting his questioning gaze. She headed through the foyer. Gavin stayed behind for a minute, then followed.

She climbed the stairs methodically. She could hear Gavin climbing two steps behind but ignored him. She wanted to tell him to stay away, but she didn't want to be alone, either.

Midway up, she stopped when she smelled the peppermint. The odor came from behind her.

Her fingers danced nervously on the banister. Gavin had stopped climbing too. He waited one step below. What did the odor mean, coming from Gavin's direction? she wondered.

"Kelly, what's wrong?"

Was the odor linked to the spirit of Miss Mary? she wondered. Then would that make Gavin—?

"Do you feel okay?" His voice betrayed genuine concern.

"Do you smell that?" she blurted out. "The peppermint?"

For a moment, he looked confused. "You mean my gum? Is it bothering you? Do you want a piece?" He slid a slim foil pack out of his back jeans pocket and held it up to her.

Kelly flushed, feeling like a fool. She noticed now that he was chewing gum. Mint gum, obviously. "No. I'm good." She continued up the last few stairs, refusing to look back at him.

At the landing, she turned left. Ryan's room was the first one. His door was closed. An old handwritten KEEP OUT sign from last summer was taped crookedly in the center.

She knocked. Twice.

Silence.

She pressed her face against the door. "Are you in there, Ryan?"

She waited. *Please,* she thought. *Please be in there.*

"I'm coming in," she warned.

She waited a moment, then pushed open the door.

The pain was immediate.

Sharp claws slashed through her sweatshirt, piercing the skin on her shoulders. She shrieked in agony. Her arms flailed frantically. She fought to release herself from the lethal grip.

And then she heard the high-pitched wail. A bone-chilling, inhuman sound like she'd never heard before.

CHAPTER 15

Was this how it was going to end for her? Had June and Paige been attacked too, before disappearing? She squeezed her eyes closed.

"Get away! Get off her!" Gavin cried. His quick hands grabbed the creature, releasing her from its painful grip.

The creature hissed violently, struggling to free itself, yowling in protest. Turning, Kelly caught a glimpse of thrashing black fur, whiskers, and bared teeth.

Ezra.

The cat must be totally spooked, Kelly thought. *Just like me.*

Gavin tossed the thrashing cat into the hallway, where it darted away, ears flattened, tail held high.

She knew she should thank him, but try as she might, she couldn't force the words out. Instead she gently rubbed her back where Ezra's claws had scratched. It throbbed slightly.

"There's some blood on your shirt. Not much. A few drops," Gavin remarked.

"It's more the sting. His claws don't cause too much damage," she said. "I've had it happen before."

"Do you want to get some Band-Aids or something? Or wash it off?"

"In a minute," she replied, suddenly remembering why she was in Ryan's room.

She lifted the light switch, and the answer was painfully obvious. Ryan wasn't here. He hadn't been here all day. The piles of clean, folded laundry his mother had set on his bed before rushing off to the airport remained undisturbed. His laptop was shut.

She swallowed hard. "If he's not here, where is he?" she cried.

"I don't know," Gavin said.

She hadn't meant to say that aloud. It hadn't been her plan to confide in Gavin.

"Ryan's your *younger* brother, right?"

She nodded. "I just don't understand. Where is he? And Chrissie? They wouldn't just leave me here, alone, unless something bad happened. Right? I mean, you don't think so, right?" She knew she was babbling, but for the moment it just felt good to have someone else there witnessing the craziness. She didn't care if it was Gavin.

"No. I don't think so," he said carefully. He eyed her with concern again, and she wondered why he wasn't looking more concerned himself. True, it wasn't his family, but his friend was gone too. "I told you what I thought, though."

She paused. "You think we did this—with the chanting and the spinning."

"I do."

"You think we brought her back. And then she . . . what?" Her voice sounded shrill even to her own ears, but she just needed him to say it—to say the outrageous things she'd been thinking.

"She was killed too young. Maybe it was an accident. Maybe it wasn't. Either way she was ticked off, you know? It wasn't fair." Gavin blinked quickly for a few seconds. "I think she's after a little justice."

"Justice?" she repeated sharply. "What's just about taking innocent people and . . . doing . . . well, I don't know what! Where *are* they?"

Gavin nervously blinked his eyes again. "I didn't say it made sense."

She looked sideways at him. "And what about you? Why are you still here . . . with me?"

"No idea." He reddened slightly, as if embarrassed. "It'll all be okay."

"Okay? Okay? You think this is okay?" She could hear herself screaming. It felt as if she were watching herself from the other side of the room. As if this scared girl were no longer connected to her. She squeezed her eyes tightly and let the waves of fear run through her body. She felt Gavin's hand lightly pat her shoulder, but she quickly pushed it away. She didn't want him touching her.

She walked across the bedroom, over to Ryan's window. She needed some space. She had to figure out what to do. She peered out. Since she'd come inside, the pace of the snow had picked up. She watched the whiteness blanket the yard, concealing all their footprints. Soon there would be no evidence that she had been there.

She would call her parents. Her dad, this time. He'd be calm and logical. He'd tell her what to do.

She glanced up. Gavin had stepped into the hall, right outside the door. He hovered in the shadows.

She reached around blindly for her cell phone. Where was it? She realized she'd left it behind in the family room.

She pushed past Gavin. She needed to get her phone and call her dad. It felt good to have a plan. Her dad would fix this. Somehow.

Gavin trailed her to the stairs. The slapping of their feet on the wood echoed throughout the quiet house. She paused halfway down, and Gavin tumbled clumsily into her. He grabbed the banister to steady himself.

"What is it?" he demanded.

"Shhhh. Listen."

They both stood silently.

Whispers. Whispered voices from down below.

Her hand gripped the banister so tightly her knuckles grew white. "Who is it?" she asked in a hushed tone.

He shrugged, leaning over to hear.

Faint whispers. In the house.

She took a tentative step. The stair beneath her creaked. She held her breath and stopped.

The voices had a rhythm. A hushed chanting. She listened hard but couldn't make out the words.

What were they chanting?

Then just as suddenly as they'd started, the whispered voices stopped.

She and Gavin waited, frozen. Silence overtook the house once again. The steady gusting of the wind was now the only background noise.

"I want to see," she declared, fear now driving her determination. "I want to see who's speaking." It suddenly seemed more important than anything to find the whispering voices. She scrambled down the stairs, no longer caring how much noise she made. Gavin followed at her heels. Rounding the front foyer, she headed back toward the kitchen and . . .

Everything plunged into total blackness.

Kelly gasped. Her heart thudded. She stood blindly, surrounded by crushing darkness.

"I think we lost the power," Gavin said quietly.

She blinked, trying to adjust her eyes to the darkness. She could hear his shallow, raspy breaths. He was so very close. Her mind flashed back to his hands reaching for Spencer's neck. Squeezing tight. His vacant gaze and strange mutterings.

Would he try to strangle her, too? Here in the dark?

She had to get away. The darkness gave him the

perfect cover to try so many horrible things. She trembled at the thought. She took tiny steps forward, reaching out her arms in search of the wall. She found it and groped along its smooth surface. Slowly she inched her way into the kitchen. Gavin trailed steadily behind her.

Suddenly his hand grabbed her shoulder, and she jumped. "Turn this way," he instructed.

"Don't touch me again," she snapped. She took a giant step away from him. She needed to keep distance between them.

"Whatever," he muttered.

I have to find a flashlight, she thought. She edged her way around the room and bumped into her mother's desk. Tracing its contours with her fingers, she located the bottom drawer and pulled out the emergency flashlight her father kept inside. With a flick of the switch, she blasted a beam of light into Gavin's surprised face.

"Whoa!" He raised his arms in mock surrender.

The melody sounded before she could answer.

She stiffened, listening to the familiar notes. The same sinister eight notes, playing again and again.

Gavin furrowed his thick eyebrows. "Weird song. The same one we heard outside."

She nodded, her eyes locating the phone in the middle of the kitchen counter. They watched the phone glow eerily in the darkness. It played the haunting ringtone over and over.

The phone definitely hadn't been there minutes earlier, when they had come in from outside. She was sure of that.

"Is it yours?" Gavin asked, his eyes trained on the phone too.

She shook her head. "Chrissie's." The phone continued to ring. A spine-tingling summons.

Together, they both stepped toward it, as if being drawn out of the depths of the ocean by a fisherman's line.

"Who's calling?" Kelly whispered. The phone pulsed with light, a tiny strobe in the blackness of the kitchen.

They bent over the counter and gazed at the illuminated caller ID screen. Neither dared touch the phone. "I don't know the number. Do you?" she asked warily.

"No."

The foreboding melody played again.

"Should I answer it?" she asked.

"Yes," he said, his eyes wide.

She wondered if she was making a huge mistake. She reached for the phone. "Hello?"

CHAPTER 16

"Hello?" she repeated into the phone.

For a moment, all she could hear was static. Then a female voice asked shakily, "Who is this?"

Kelly hesitated. She didn't know what to say. Gavin leaned annoyingly close, blatantly curious. She turned slightly, facing the refrigerator, resting the flashlight on the counter. "It's Kelly. Who's this?"

"It's Paige."

"Paige! Is it really you?" Kelly cried. An injection of relief spread through her veins.

"Yes. It is."

"I am so, so happy. I've been searching everywhere for you!" The words flew from her mouth. "Wow! You're okay!"

"I'm sorry."

"Sorry? Why are you sorry?" Kelly asked. She smiled at Gavin and mouthed, "It's Paige!"

He nodded.

"Paige. Paige?" Kelly said into the phone, when her friend didn't answer. "Are you okay? Where are you?"

"No, I'm not." Paige's voice sounded tight. Unnatural.

"What's going on?" The happy warmth of just seconds ago grew cold. "You don't sound like you."

"I need help." The words drew out of her slowly.

"Paige, what's wrong? You're scaring me." Kelly's voice quivered. "Please, tell me."

"She's here."

"Who?" Kelly cried, squeezing the phone in frustration.

"She has me trapped," Paige explained in a hollow tone.

"Who does? Where?"

A burst of static obscured the line, muffling Paige's reply.

"Paige, I didn't hear you! Where are you?" Kelly screamed, pronouncing each word so Paige could better understand.

"I'm in your basement."

Paige was here? In her own house?

"Help me." Paige's voice now a lifeless monotone. "Save me from her. Hurry."

"You're really in my—"

The line cut off.

"Paige? Paige, are you still there?" Kelly didn't bother to hide her desperation.

No answer. Paige was gone.

On the glowing touchpad, she quickly found redial and pressed. She listened as the numbers clicked in. Ringing. The phone kept ringing. Paige wasn't picking up.

Or couldn't pick up.

Someone was down there with her.

Kelly cradled the purple phone in her palm, testing its weight as if checking to be sure it was real. She began to rock slowly. Heel to toe. Back and forth. The rhythm soothed her, allowing her to block all the jumbled thoughts. Heel to toe. Back and forth.

"Where is she?" Gavin asked. He'd picked the flashlight up off the counter and was now shining the light at her face. "Are you okay?"

She stopped rocking and shielded her eyes from the spotlight with her free hand. Her gaze darted toward the door by the desk, hidden in the darkness. "She says she's down there. In the basement."

"So let's go." He turned toward the door.

"No." She reached out and actually touched his arm to stop him.

"Huh? Why?" Shadows danced across his confused face.

"She's not alone. Someone is with her. Someone has her trapped."

"But shouldn't we help her?" Gavin asked. For the first time, she heard panic in his voice.

"Yes, but . . ." One big part of her wanted to race across the kitchen and fling open that door and pull her friend to safety. But then there was that other part of her. The part that had listened to countless "never open the door to strangers" lectures from her parents, the part that had seen those late-night scary movies where opening a door meant walking right into evil, and the part that was *scared*.

Her thoughts were interrupted as a strange whirring that filled the kitchen. Then a beep. And another. In a rush, the lights flooded on and the appliances came back to life.

In the brightness, she immediately knew what to do. Paige was her best friend. She *had* to help her.

She moved quickly to the basement door.

"So we're going down?" Gavin asked, his voice loud. He stood by her side.

"Shh," she warned. "And yes." She had decided.

She peered at the crack at the bottom of the door. No light seeped out of it. The basement was dark, even with the power back on. Her hand rested on the door-knob.

Fear overcame her. She couldn't turn it. What was she walking into? Was she being stupid? Anything could be waiting for her behind that door.

"Weapon," she whispered. "We need a weapon."

Her eyes scanned the area by them. An umbrella stood propped by the back door. It was pointy but seemed silly. She knew there were mops and brooms in the cleaning closet off the back mudroom leading to the garage, but she couldn't imagine what good those would do. She had no idea what she was looking for.

Gavin raised his eyebrows. "You—you think we'll need a weapon?" he stammered.

"I don't know what we'll need," she shot back, her anxiety peaking. "I don't know who is down there."

"Or if it's human," he added quietly.

She froze. He had that intense, disturbing look again. She edged away.

She glanced down at Chrissie's phone, still cradled in her left hand. She pushed the keypad, and it blinked to life. Carefully she dialed the numbers 9-1-1.

Positioning her left thumb over the send button just in case, she twisted the knob. The basement door swung open, and she stepped down into the darkness.

CHAPTER 17

She tentatively took the first step. Her stomach twisted, and she paused. Was she really doing this?

Yes. Yes, she was. She had to help Paige. And Paige might know where her brother was, and Chrissie, and everyone else. *Come on, Kelly,* she coached herself.

Her hand reached for the light switch, but before she could touch it, the lights flashed on themselves and then—

"Surprise!"

Kelly screamed and reeled backward. She dropped the cell phone and frantically reached for the banister. Her knees wobbled from the shock. What was going on?

"Surprise!" the voices yelled again.

She stared dumbfounded at the smiling faces beaming

up at her from the bottom of the stairs. Paige, June, Spencer, Chrissie, Ryan, Spencer's mom, and his brother, Charlie.

"Wh-what?" She couldn't understand what they were all doing in her basement. Together. Looking so . . . happy.

"Happy birthday!" they all cried.

Her brain took a few seconds to compute the meaning of what was going on. Then she noticed the balloons and streamers decorating the usually blah basement.

"Go downstairs." Gavin gave her a gentle nudge from behind.

She glanced over her shoulder and gave him a questioning look. She still was too scared and confused to speak.

"It's a surprise party," he explained. "For your birthday."

"Really?" Her voice came out as a squeak. "Seriously?"

Gavin smiled widely. "Seriously." She noticed that it was the first time she'd seen him smile. His face looked different now. Warmer. Friendlier.

"Get down here!" June commanded good-naturedly. She hurried up the stairs and grabbed Kelly's hand. Kelly let June lead her. She stood surrounded by her friends.

"I had no idea . . ." Her voice trailed off, still amazed.

137

"Of course, silly," Paige teased. "That's why it's called a *surprise* party."

"We have cupcakes." Charlie, wearing his truck-printed pajamas, tugged at Kelly's pant leg. "And they're chocolate!"

She looked down at him and rumpled his staticky brown hair. "Really? I love cupcakes."

"Sit down, birthday girl," Mrs. Stone, Spencer's mom, said. She led the group to the sofa. Kelly sank into the cushions, letting her body relax for the first time in hours. She took in the display of cupcakes, chips and dip, and hot chocolate on the table in front of them.

"This is amazing." She looked at all her friends, no longer in pajamas but in warm winter clothes, gathered around. Then her eyes stopped at Chrissie, all happy and bubbly. "Wait. I don't get it. You were outside. And then you weren't. And you were acting all strange and wouldn't answer when I called you. . . ." Her gaze moved to Ryan, smirking as he shoved a cupcake into his mouth. "Hey, and you! Why wouldn't you answer me? I was so scared."

"Gotcha!" everyone shrieked at once.

"Huh?" Kelly said.

"We totally scared you," Spencer explained. "You're no

longer the Master of Scares, are you? You were *terrified*."

"We got you good!" Paige sang out, bouncing from foot to foot gleefully.

A joke. It was all a joke, Kelly now realized.

She nodded slowly. "Oh, wow. I was so freaked out." She thought back over the events of the night. "So it was all fake?"

"Yep," June said, sitting next to her. "And you fell for it all."

"I'm a good actor, aren't I?" Chrissie beamed proudly.

"Not as good as I am!" Ryan countered.

"Hey, I taught you everything you know. Who showed you how to do the zombie stare? I'm so good, I should open an acting school," Chrissie bragged.

"But I don't understand. . . ." Kelly tried to quickly tie all the pieces together but couldn't.

"When we saw how bummed you were at not having a party tonight, we came up with the idea of a surprise party. I told Chrissie, and she was cool with it," Paige explained. "She clued in Ryan."

"Then we decided that it was time to scare the Master of Scares," Spencer continued. "But it was Ryan who came up with the most genius idea."

Kelly stared at her little brother. He gloated and reached for his second cupcake. "How?" she asked.

"He showed me the article you were reading earlier about Mary Owens," Chrissie said. "Before the sleepover even started, we came up with a plan."

"We pretended that the summoning of Miss Mary worked," June added.

"Wait, so you didn't see anyone behind me?" Kelly asked.

"Of course not," June scoffed. "And then we started disappearing. Me first. Spencer found this program that made our screens turn that wacky red. Scared you, right?"

"Yeah," she admitted. "But who was Chrissie talking to on the phone?" She turned to the older girl. "You know, when you were acting all sad and weird."

"I should get an Academy Award, don't you think?" Chrissie beamed. "I was talking to Paige. Totally made all that stuff up to play with your mind."

"Actually, I was more awesome. Right, Kel?" Ryan asked. "I mean, you so fell for my zombie routine."

She punched him playfully on the arm. "That was so mean!"

Ryan laughed, and Kelly looked around the room.

That was when she noticed Gavin, standing slightly behind the others. "How does Gavin fit in? I mean, no offense, but I barely even know you."

"That was perfect, I must say." Spencer grinned, clearly pleased with himself. "I had invited Gav to stay over before I even knew about this whole webcam thing. His dad and brother had to go out of town. Anyway, we decided that since you didn't really know him, he could totally mess with you. We really wanted you to believe he was possessed."

"I believed that," she agreed.

Gavin chuckled, and Kelly cringed. "Sorry. You were way creepy. Especially when you came running out of the bushes. What was that about?"

"That wasn't planned," Spencer admitted. "You see, we each made our way over here, one by one, and sneaked into the basement through the side door, so you wouldn't hear us enter the house. Chrissie unlocked it for us. Charlie heard about it and really wanted to come too. And my mom wouldn't let us do all this without an adult, so that's why she is here." Spencer grimaced.

"I played along, but I was always looking out for you, Kelly honey," Mrs. Stone said. Her pale-blue eyes twinkled. Clearly she'd enjoyed herself.

Chrissie took over. "I made the boot prints to nowhere. Then I doubled back on the same prints—not easy, if you want to know—and hid in the mudroom off the kitchen to watch you. But when I saw you wandering aimlessly in the storm outside at night, well, I got scared that you would get hurt or frostbitten or something. We knew we had to get you back inside and to the party."

"So you sent Gavin after me?" she asked.

"Yeah," Gavin continued. "I snuck back out the side door and into the backyard. My appearing was creepy and still kept you scared. I really didn't mean to chase you like that, but when you just took off, I had no choice." He grinned. "You're fast. And boy, was it cold out there."

"And then?" Kelly asked, still working overtime to connect the dots.

"Well, I wasn't expecting the cat attack, that's for sure!"

Ryan and her friends laughed. Ezra's flying leaps were legendary.

"But I did manage to get you to the basement," Gavin explained.

"It helped that I called you," Paige interjected. "I used Mrs. Stone's phone. I figured there was no way you'd recognize her cell number on the caller ID."

Kelly shook her head. "Not at all. You sounded so . . . scared."

"Chrissie's not the only actor in the family, right?" Paige grinned; then her face softened. "And, hey, it's nice to know you'd come save me. You know, if anything ever happened for real."

"Of course," Kelly murmured, nodding at her friend.

"And that's the whole story," June concluded.

"Wow." She was completely in awe. She thought through their complicated plans, then smiled. "I've taught you all well. Good scare. No, excellent scare!"

"Ha-ha," Ryan said, smirking. "You'd think—"

Everyone stopped speaking as the familiar ringtone sounded. Instinctively Kelly froze, still freaked out by the haunting melody. Why was the haunting melody playing again? Her eyes darted about the basement.

Charlie jumped from the sofa and ran to the top of the stairs. He scooped up the little purple phone from where it had fallen on the landing. "Phone's ringing!" he called.

"Give it here." Chrissie hurried over to him.

"The creepy ringtone?" Kelly asked.

"Just put there to mess with you," Paige explained. "Good, huh?"

Kelly exhaled. She had the feeling it would take her a while to stop jumping at every little thing. "Ooh, look. Presents," she cried, suddenly noticing the little pile of packages alongside the sofa.

"Hi, Mrs. Garcia. How are you?" Kelly heard Chrissie greet her mother. "Everything's great here. Storm? Well, it's snowing a lot and all, but it isn't bothering us. We're having a great time." Chrissie smiled down at Kelly and her friends.

Kelly smiled back and began ripping open the gold wrapping paper on a little package. "This is the best birthday surprise ever," she announced. "Even if you all did scare me half to death."

It was after eleven when Spencer, Gavin, and Mrs. Stone, carrying sleeping Charlie, crossed the snowy street to return home. June and Paige trudged over to Paige's house. It was decided that June would spend the night there. The snow was too deep to even walk around the block.

Kelly yawned as she finally pulled open her dresser

drawer for a fresh pair of pajamas. A flash of black fur flew through the air, and she sucked in her breath. Ezra leaped off the top of the dresser once again and scurried out of her bedroom into the dark hallway.

"Good idea!" Kelly called after the cat. "Go bother Ryan."

She was exhausted. Her brother and Chrissie had already gone to sleep. She pulled back her plaid comforter and crawled into her warm bed. Even though the heat had miraculously turned back on, it was still cold upstairs. She snuggled into the sheets and smiled at how badly her friends had scared her. She still had trouble believing it was all a joke.

Rolling onto her side, she turned off her bedside lamp. The darkness was welcome for the first time today. She felt as if she'd come off the school bus a year ago. She groaned as she rolled back over and saw the glow. She stared at the greenish light of her laptop perched on her desk. She didn't feel like getting up. But she knew she should turn it off.

She pulled herself out of bed and wandered over to her desk. Resting her fingers on the keyboard, she squinted at the screen. Their webcam conference session from earlier was still up and running. Spencer and

Gavin's frame still appeared on her monitor.

Her friends, of course, weren't at their computers. The *Avatar* poster behind Spencer's desk filled the screen. Shadows covered the room. Spencer and Gavin were probably asleep.

She paused before logging off. Then she smiled slyly. She'd send an e-mail to the boys. A little something spooky to wake up to. Her fingers began to type.

MISS MARY. MISS MARY. MISS MARY.

She chanted the words under her breath as she typed. She was about to hit send when she glanced up. Her breath caught in her throat.

There, in the corner of Spencer's screen, a figure shimmered. A woman in the shadows. Reaching out. Reaching out to her.

The figure moved closer, gliding toward the screen.

Red dress. Translucent skin pulled tight over protruding bones. A skeletal hand reaching out. Pushing up against the screen, scratching and clawing as if trying to get through. To get out. To escape.

Kelly whimpered, then sucked in her breath. She slammed her finger against the power button on the side of the laptop. In a moment, her screen turned dark.

The ghostly figure was gone.

She remained motionless in her chair. She stared at the screen. Her heart pounded. Had she seen what she thought she'd seen? She shook her head. She couldn't have. It had been a long night. She was overtired. That was it. Definitely overtired.

She inhaled deeply. She had to calm down. Breathe. She had to breathe. She exhaled and then breathed in again. And began to shake.

Peppermint.

The overpowering scent of peppermint. The odor came from her computer. As if it was flowing out of the screen!

She couldn't stop shaking.

The smell. It was so strong.

She thought back on the night. She had never told her friends about smelling the peppermint. And now she realized with horror that they had never mentioned it either. The aroma surrounded her, invading her throat, her nose.

She thought about the words she'd just typed to Spencer.

MISS MARY.

DO NOT FEAR—
WE HAVE ANOTHER CREEPY TALE FOR YOU!

CONTINUE READING FOR A SNEAK PEEK AT

You're invited to a

CREEPOVER™

The Show Must Go On!

THIRTY YEARS AGO . . .

"You're fired, Ms. Wormhouse!" barked the principal of Thomas Jefferson Middle School. "And we are canceling your play, forever." He leaned forward on his desk and locked his piercing gaze on the eyes of the woman seated across from him.

Mildred P. Wormhouse stared back, her dark, sunken eyes blazing with anger. "Canceling?" she barked. "I've worked on this play my entire life. Fire me if you wish, but the play will be performed!" Her curly shock of jet-black hair shook with every word.

"Maybe somewhere else," the principal said, standing now, his tone growing increasingly impatient. "But it will not be performed here, at this school—ever! Do you have such little regard for human life?"

"Bah!" Wormhouse snarled with a dismissive gesture. She stood, her long black coat flapping near her ankles as she turned away from the principal.

"A girl died last night, Ms. Wormhouse," the principal said through clenched teeth. "On this school's stage, playing the lead in the play you wrote and directed. And that was only the final terrible incident. The rehearsals have been marred with accidents and other troubles. In fact, strange things have been happening at this school since the day you arrived. I've heard rumors that your play is cursed. I'm not a superstitious man, but I'm starting to believe them. I've seen to it that every last copy of the play has been thrown out."

Wormhouse turned slowly back toward the principal. "Cursed?" she hissed, her lips curling in a slight smile. "You really shouldn't let your fears get the best of you—"

"This conversation is over," the principal interrupted. He marched across the room and threw the door open. A roar erupted from the angry mob of parents and teachers who had gathered outside the office.

"There she is!" one man shouted.

"It's her fault," a woman yelled. "Her play!"

Wormhouse squirmed out the door and through the crowd; her head bent low, her black coat flapping with every step like a cape. She headed for a hallway that led to the front door of the school. Pausing, she turned back toward the irate crowd.

"You may fire me," Wormhouse cried. "But you cannot stop my play. It will be performed." Then she turned down the hall toward the front door of the building.

"Good riddance!" someone in the mob shouted.

"Don't ever show your face around here again!" screamed someone else.

Wormhouse disappeared from view around a corner in the hallway. But instead of turning left toward the front door, she turned right—toward the school's auditorium, where her play had opened last night and where the girl playing the lead had died.

Walking quickly down the center aisle of the empty auditorium, glancing back over her shoulder every few steps, Wormhouse made her way backstage. Spotting an old steamer trunk, she shoved a pile of costumes off the top, then yanked open the lid. Inside the trunk were props from all the years of school productions. She reached into an inner pocket of her long coat and pulled out the last remaining copy of her play. Burying it beneath the mound of props inside the trunk, she gently lowered the lid.

Seething, her breath now labored, she repeated her vow, muttering to herself, "The show must go on."

PRESENT DAY . . .

Felix Gomez had been the drama teacher at the school for a few years now, and he really wanted to do something different this year. He would put on a new play. . . .

WANT MORE CREEPINESS?

Then you're in luck, because P. J. Night has some more scares for you and your friends!

Kelly searches for her friends all over her house, but doesn't find them until the very end. P. J. Night wants to know . . . are you a better detective? Find all 30 words in this word search! Words can appear up, down, backward, forward, or diagonally.

BASEMENT	ICICLE	PHONE
BURIED	JUNE	PIZZA
CHARLIE	KELLY	POSSESSED
CHRISSIE	LAPTOP	RYAN
DARKNESS	MISS MARY	SCARE
EZRA	NEWSPAPER	SLEEPOVER
FOOTPRINT	PAIGE	SNOW
GAVIN	PARKA	SPENCER
GHOST	PEPPERMINT	VERMONT
HAUNTING	PHILLY	WEBCAM

READY TO SOLVE?
WE DARE YOU!

```
V H X E K E L L Y I T N I R P T O O F Y
A E G T N E M E S A B W E P A R K A S A
R C W B Z H X D S G Y D U Z R Y F H D T
Y L L I H P Q F F G O E E C P A I G E H
S I A I E D S B C V Z C U I O N U U X Y
A T R B P V R G M R Z T Z H S P L L U G
X E N U J P Y I A X M Z H O S C A R E O
B I N K Q T I B C V A F D J E N K O T P
H S S I I P C S B L I P K J S X C Q I E
R S R E E F I X E M A N H W S N I M N P
B I G D A L C O W N M M A S E N G I P P
C R Q F V F L M R W T N U F D E V S J E
G H O S T Z E E U M T O N E K W R S W R
T C S R Z Q V E R M O N T I L S Y M B M
C T N T F O A L U L R A I L K P M A A I
Q W X T P Q W P P D B N N R E A H R W N
P M S E Q L T O K L T K G A E P J Y S T
W J E O D A R K N E S S R H P E U V K W
C L E X D R Q J K S P E N C E R B W J V
S K L Y M L A P T O P H O N E V I T E E
```

DID YOU FIND ALL 30 WORDS?
FIND THE ANSWER KEY IN THE FOLLOWING PAGES.

YOU'RE INVITED TO . . .
CREATE YOUR OWN SCARY STORY!

Do you want to turn your sleepover into a creepover? Telling a spooky story is a great way to set the mood. P. J. Night has written a few sentences to get you started. Fill in the rest of the story on the lines provided and have fun scaring your friends.

You can also collaborate with your friends on this story by taking turns. Have everyone at your sleepover sit in a circle. Pick one person to start. She will add a sentence or two to the story, cover what she wrote with a piece of paper, leaving only the last word or phrase visible, and then pass the story to the next girl. Once everyone has taken a turn, read the scary story you created together aloud!

My last vacation was hardly a vacation—it was more like a nightmare. What had been advertised as a gorgeous hotel looked more like the set of a horror film. The windows shook in the wind, and the rooms smelled old and musty. When we ate dinner in the dining room, I kept expecting the chandelier to crash down from the ceiling and a skeleton to pop out of the closet. And things went from bad to a lot worse when I excused myself only to get lost on my way to the bathroom. I opened the wrong door and walked straight into . . .

_____

_____

_____

_____

_____

_____

_____

_____

_____

_____

_____

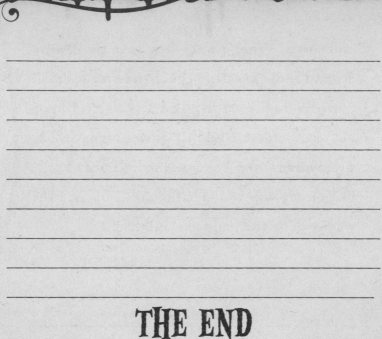

THE END

THE ANSWERS YOU SEEK ARE BELOW:

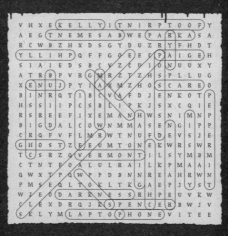

A lifelong night owl, **P. J. NIGHT** often works furiously into the wee hours of the morning, writing down spooky tales and dreaming up new stories of the supernatural and otherworldly. Although P. J.'s whereabouts are unknown at this time, we suspect the author lives in a drafty, old mansion where the floorboards creak when no one is there and the flickering candlelight creates shadows that creep along the walls. We truly wish we could tell you more, but we've been sworn to keep P. J.'s identity a secret . . . and it's a secret we will take to our graves!

What's better than reading a really spooky story?

Writing your own!

You just read a great book. It gave you ideas, didn't it? Ideas for your next story: characters...plot...setting... You can't wait to grab a notebook and a pen and start writing it all down.

It happens a lot. *Ideas just pop into your head.* In between classes entire story lines take shape in your imagination. And when you start writing, the words flow, and you end up with notebooks crammed with your creativity.

It's okay, you aren't alone. Come to **KidPub**, the web's largest gathering of kids just like you. Share your stories with thousands of people from all over the world. Meet new friends and see what they're writing. Test your skills in one of our writing contests. See what other kids think about your stories.

And above all, *come to write!*

www.KidPub.com